The Cross of Victory

by

Dr. Rocco Leonard Martino

A Division of Chesapeake Bay Media, LLC

(c) Copyright 2016 by Dr. Rocco Leonard Martino.
All rights reserved worldwide.

ISBN: 0983564922
ISBN-13: 9780983564928

All rights reserved. No part of this book shall be reproduced or transmitted in any form or by any means, electronic, mechanical, magnetic, and photographic, including photocopying, recording or by any information storage and retrieval system, without prior written permission of the publisher. No patent liability is assumed with respect to the use of the information contained herein. Although every precaution has been taken in the preparation of this book, the publisher and author assume no responsibility for errors or omissions. Neither is any liability assumed for damages resulting from the use of the information contained herein.

Please visit: www.bluenosepress.com

Published by:

BlueNose Press, Inc.
A Division of Chesapeake Bay Media, LLC
Printed in the United States of America
Published January, 2016

Works by Rocco Leonard Martino

Fiction
The Cross of Victory
Christianity: A Criminal Investigation...
The Resurrection: A Criminal Investigation...
9-11-11: The Tenth Anniversary Attack
The Plot to Cancel Christmas

Radio Drama
X the Unknown: There is no Christ in Christmas

Nonfiction
Memories: Volume I - Stories for My Grandchildren
Memories: Volume II - Scientist and Writer
Memories: Volume III - Changing the World
Rocket Ships and God
Walking Around the Neighborhood
People, Machines, and Politics of the Cyber Age Creation
Essays Along the Way
Finding the Critical Path
Applied Operational Planning
Allocating and Scheduling Resources
Critical Path Networks
Resources Management
Dynamic Costing
Project Management
Decision Patterns

Decision Tables with Staff of MDI
Information Management
Integrated Manufacturing Systems
Management Information Systems
MIS Methodology
Personnel Management Systems
Computer-R-Age with Webster V. Allen
IMPACT 70s with John Gentile
UNIVAC Operations Manual
Ground Effect of Radio Wave Propagation
Heat Transfer in Slip Flow

Reviews of
The Cross of Victory

"What a marvelous book. A complete contextualization of the passion, trial, and death of Jesus. Every Christian and, indeed, everyone should read it. Though known in many small pieces, putting them into a complete story, gives new insight. The portrayal of Judas is especially compelling."
   - **John J. Schrems, Ph.D., Professor Emeritus of English, University of Pennsylvania**

Debating the question: What is the root of all evil? Many, based on experience and Scripture, decide on pride. Fundamental to pride is the unwillingness to accept the truth about ourselves or the world in which God has placed us. Jesus said to his fellow Jews: "The truth will make you free." Jesus said to Pilate: "Everyone who is of the truth hears my voice." Pilate seated before the Word of God asked, "What is truth?" Using the canvas of an historical novel, *"The Cross of Victory,"* Dr. Martino has masterfully painted a compelling picture of how perpetrators of the consummate evil, especially the Chief Priest, Caiaphas, came to believe their own lies. Consequently this book is not as entertaining as it is psychologically enlightening; it is thought provoking and spiritually rewarding. The victory of the Cross is truly the triumph of truth over the Devil, a murderer from the beginning, a

liar and the father of lies. Refer to John 8:31-59 and 18:37-38.
> - ***Paul Peterson, Professor Emeritus of Theology, Archdiocese of Philadelphia***

As I concluded reading Rocco Leonard Martino's third religious novel, *"The Cross of Victory"*, I was struck with amazement at this latest novel. He writes with glorious words, a profound mind, and a heart touched with grace, faith and powerful love that only God can reveal.

Dr. Martino's newest religious novel reveals his own heart, it will touch people in this needy world that we live in. I applaud this victory!
> - ***Rev. George Aschenbrenner, S.J., Jesuit Center, Wernersville, Pennsylvania; Rector Emeritus, University of Scranton***

Of course, most, if not all of us, know the story. Jesus is tried, tortured, put to death, but rises from the dead on the third day. In this novel, *The Cross of Victory,* however, we are taken further and deeper into the Passion of Christ. Drawing on his years of prayer and meditation, on his own experiences of living in the human family, Dr. Martino has given us insights into the political realities that created the environment necessary to condemn Jesus to death. Dr. Martino infuses the characters involved in the Passion of Christ with all too recognizable characteristics, from the fidelity of Joseph or Arimathea, and Nicodemus to the perfidious behavior of Caiaphas and Annas and the weakness of Judas and Pilate.

He traces Caiaphas' terror of losing power, his inordinate jealousy of Jesus' relationship with people: "...I would especially like to find evidence to prove Jesus blasphemed so we can condemn him to death...He must be removed. If He is not, he will continue in His popularity... and pose a significant threat to our authority," Thus Caiaphas exercises the best in the toolbox of the morally corrupt-manipulation- to persuade the unfortunate, weak Judas to help. But one manipulation won't do it. Pilate, who understands the workings of the Sanhedrin leadership, yet is ever eager not to displease his Roman superiors, also succumbs to the web of lies. Dr. Martino, it seems to me, and with good reason, is less condemnatory and even shows a touch of sympathy toward Judas and Pilate. In fact, one is tempted to ask, "What, in a similar situation would I have done? What, in a similar situation would happen in the twenty-first century? Political corruption and manipulation didn't end with the end of the Roman Empire and the power of the Sanhedrin.

Dr. Martino treats the Passion and the death of Jesus realistically, but not so graphically that it is bone chilling. He describes it with respectful dignity and with historical and biological accuracy. Our hearts, minds and imaginations are engaged in the pain and ignominy of Christ's suffering; added to this is the description of His mother's pain. As the onset of His condemnation becomes inevitable, Mary cries and sobs. This may not appear in these words in Scripture, but for a mother to do otherwise is unthinkable. Again, through his years of prayer and meditation, Dr. Martino can understand and envision this.

The novel ends quickly and dramatically—in a chapter of four short paragraphs, as Jesus appears to Mary Magdalene. Only three words from Mary to Jesus are needed to understand that Cross has indeed become Victory. "You are Risen!"

It is Advent, quite close to Christmas, as this review is being written; the novel is as inspiring and relevant now as it will be during the Lenten season. The reader will find an appeal both to mind and to heart in the story of our Redemption.

- ***Sr. Joan Dugan, S.S.J., English Instructor for Secondary Schools in the Archdiocese of Philadelphia, the Diocese of Harrisburg, and the Diocese of Allentown***

Table of Contents

Preface and Acknowledgements	1
Dedication	7
Chapter One	9
The Threat to Jesus	
Chapter Two	17
The Search for a Traitor	
Chapter Three	21
Fulfillment of the Covenant	
Chapter Four	
The Entry into Jerusalem	
Chapter Five	33
Jesus, a Threat to the Civil Order	
Chapter Six	41
Jesus in the Temple	
Chapter Seven	49
The Betrayal Plot	
Chapter Eight	55
Pontius Pilate	
Chapter Nine	61
Caiaphas Plants the Seed	
Chapter Ten	67
The Supper	
Chapter Eleven	77
The Arrest	
Chapter Twelve	81
Trial Before the Sanhedrin	
Chapter Thirteen	87
Caiaphas Plotting the Execution of Jesus	

Chapter Fourteen	**91**
The First Trial before Pontius Pilate	
Chapter Fifteen	**95**
Herod Antipas, Tetrarch of Galilee	
Chapter Sixteen	**101**
The Final Trial before Pilate	
Chapter Seventeen	**109**
Condemned!	
Chapter Eighteen	**115**
Informing the Disciples	
Chapter Nineteen	**119**
Via Dolorosa	
Chapter Twenty	**125**
Crucifixion	
Chapter Twenty-One	**131**
The Wake	
Chapter Twenty-Two	**139**
Jesus is Risen!	
Reviews of *The Resurrection*	**141**
Reviews of *Christianity*	**147**

Preface and Acknowledgements

We all face death. It has a finality to it. Most of us pray for a happy death--a death free of pain, mental anguish, and fear. Can you imagine the anguish and pain experienced by Jesus as He was unjustly arrested, unjustly tried, flogged to within an inch of His life, crowned with thorns that pierced His brow, and forced to carry His own cross before He was nailed to it. And yet, in all of this, He stood erect, praying that God the Father would forgive those who were torturing Him since they did not know what they were doing. He thought of others, not of Himself. He tried to console the women as He walked to Calvary. From the cross He tried to console His mother, and asked John to take care of her, and she of him. From the cross, he pardoned a criminal on one side. Had the other criminal also asked for forgiveness, he too would have been pardoned. Throughout His ordeal Jesus thought not of Himself, but of others.

That is what I tried to portray in this book.

I entitled this book *The Cross of Victory*. My objective was to stress the fact that the crucifixion was not the end but only the portal to the resurrection which is the beginning. Jesus allowed Himself to be brutalized and to be crucified as a symbol to us of the meaning of His life. He gave of Himself for us. His was the supreme sacrifice, not a failure, not a tragedy, but the opening to the resurrection which is the glorious conquest of death.

The resurrection is the promise of eternal life for all of us. Hence I thought it fitting to call this book, *The Cross of Victory*. I tried to maintain close affinity to the scriptures in writing this book. The words attributed to Jesus at all times were taken from one of the Gospels by Matthew, Mark, Luke, or John. During the Passion itself, I tended to rely more on John whom I knew was a witness to it. The chapter associated with the anointing of the body and the burial of Jesus in the tomb is not in the scriptures. There are statements that He was taken down from the cross and placed in the tomb. And yet, I could visualize the scene that I portrayed in that chapter.

It is difficult to imagine the depravity of character of Caiaphas and Annas which blinded them to the majesty and nobility of Jesus; and blinded them to the importance of His message. One would hope that they finally accepted the truth. Jesus did indeed rise from the dead. The proof is incontestable. I covered that in a previous novel, *The Resurrection: A Criminal Investigation of the Mysterious Disappearance of the Body of Crucified Criminal Jesus of Nazareth*.

Historically, even afterwards, Caiaphas continued to persecute the followers of Jesus. James, the head of the church in Jerusalem, was executed on orders from Caiaphas. Closer to the crucifixion of Jesus, Stephen was stoned, once again at the instigation of Caiaphas.

It is the resurrection which is this climax of the journey of Jesus on Earth. His human nature was crucified, died, and was buried; but His divine nature rose from the dead to create the foundation for Christianity. Christianity is a religion of hope. It is the epitomized theme "do not be afraid" in the major book

THE CROSS OF VICTORY

by Pope Saint John Paul II, *Crossing the Threshold of Hope*.

It is the Nicene Creed* which spells out, in summary detail, the belief of Christians.

> I believe in one God, the Father almighty, maker of heaven and earth, of all things visible and invisible.
>
> I believe in one Lord Jesus Christ, the Only Begotten Son of God, born of the Father before all ages. God from God, Light from Light, true God from true God, begotten, not made, consubstantial with the Father; through him all things were made.
>
> For us men and for our salvation he came down from heaven, and by the Holy Spirit was incarnate of the Virgin Mary, and became man.
>
> For our sake he was crucified under Pontius Pilate, he suffered death and was buried, and rose again on the third day in accordance with the Scriptures.
>
> He ascended into heaven and is seated at the right hand of the Father. He will come again in glory to judge the living and the dead and his kingdom will have no end.
>
> I believe in the Holy Spirit, the Lord, the giver of life, who proceeds from the Father and the Son,

who with the Father and the Son is adored and glorified, who has spoken through the prophets.

I believe in one, holy, catholic and apostolic Church. I confess one Baptism for the forgiveness of sins and I look forward to the resurrection of the dead and the life of the world to come.

Amen.

*The Nicene Creed was formulated at the council of Nicea, 325 AD. It may be found on the web at http://www.usccb.org/beliefs-and-teachings/what-we-believe/

This book, *The Cross of Victory*, completes my trilogy on Jesus. The first was *The Resurrection: A Criminal Investigation of the Mysterious Disappearance of the Body of Crucified Criminal Jesus of Nazareth*, which came as a result of a challenge from my son, Paul, to write a definitive book about the resurrection. After a great deal of thought I decided to do this as a novel, close to the facts connecting the missing episodes which must have occurred with dialogue true to the characters speaking.
    The second was *Christianity: A Criminal Investigation of the Motivation, Structure, Growth, and Threat to Rome*. This book too, was put in the guise of a novel, and analyzed the factors which led to the explosive growth of Christianity.
    This book, *The Cross of Victory,* was my attempt to show the nobility of character of Jesus, and His divine

nature as the human nature was subjected to horrible torture. The climax of the crucifixion, of course, is the resurrection; which is the triumph over death. The Cross, then, is a symbol of Victory—victory over death, victory over evil, victory over sin.

    No book of this nature could be written without help. I am grateful to Jordan Hadaway for her transcription of my dictations and for her editing of the text. Publication of this book wouldn't have been possible without the efforts of my son Joseph, for proofreading, editing and re-editing this book, as well as designing the covers and preparing the text for production. His attention to detail is unparalleled by many "professionals" in the industry. Biblical quotations were taken from The Zondervan Corporation, LLC.

Rocco Leonard Martino
Villanova, Pennsylvania
January 15, 2016

ROCCO LEONARD MARTINO

Dedication

This book may very well be my last. I dedicate it to my immediate family, most especially my wife, Barbara, and to all those who stood by me and helped in so many ways during my long battle with bladder cancer. God bless you.

Rocco Leonard Martino
Villanova, Pennsylvania
January 15, 2016

ROCCO LEONARD MARTINO

Chapter One
The Threat to Jesus

Nicodemus and Joseph had been friends for many years. They were both also friends of Jesus, the carpenter and itinerant preacher from Nazareth.

They had many things in common. They lived close by each other, thought alike, and were both members of the Sanhedrin.

The Sanhedrin was the council that regulated Jewish religion, and as such, to a large extent, the daily lives of the Jews. It was composed of the Chief Priests and priests of the Temple, the most learned men in the scriptures. The total number was seventy-one so that all decisions would be final, a simple majority being sufficient even to condemn someone to death.

The Sanhedrin had the power of life and death, the power to collect taxes, the power to set rates of transfer in the Temple, and was the final court of adjudication of any transgressions against the Jewish law.

The Sanhedrin was made up of two groups of people, the Sadducees and the Pharisees. Both Nicodemus and Joseph of Arimathea were Pharisees. Sadducees and Pharisees differed only with regard to belief[1] in an afterlife. The Sadducees had no such belief, whereas the Pharisees did. The Sadducees controlled the Sanhedrin.

The head of the Sanhedrin was the Chief Priest who was appointed by the Romans. At that time the Chief Priest was Caiaphas, the son-in-law of a former Chief

---

[1] They were "sad, you see."

Priest, Annas. Annas had five sons all of whom had been Chief Priests. Annas had been the Chief Priest for ten years before he was deposed by the Romans almost twenty years ago. He still exerted a significant amount of influence, in spite of not being officially the Chief Priest. To a large extent, he acted as if he were. Annas benefited largely in a financial way from the transactions that occurred in the Temple. These transactions were the conversion of ordinary money into the money of the Temple, the Tyre, and then in transactions using Tyres to purchase items for sacrifice, such as young lambs.

The current Chief Priest, Caiaphas, was concerned about the rumors associated with the influence of Jesus, a traveling preacher who had suddenly burst upon the scene.

During the past three years this Jesus, with no formal Rabbinical training, had travelled throughout Judea, disputed with Rabbis in the Synagogue, countered the arguments of Sadducees and Pharisees in the public square, cured myriad people of their diseases, and created a vast throng of followers. He had not only cured the blind and given them sight, and made the crippled from birth stand up to walk, but He had even raised the dead to life on at least three occasions. He had fed thousands of His followers with five loaves of bread and two fishes. He had never been perceived as a threat to the status quo in Judea. He preached a message of repentance and forgiveness. If anything, He was an instrument for peace and certainly no threat to the civil order. Jesus was very popular with the masses. For those same reasons, the Chief Priest considered Jesus a major threat to his power and influence.

During His ministry years, Jesus had come to know and befriend Nicodemus and Joseph of Arimathea. They had learned that Jesus was traveling from Capernaum to Bethany on His way to Jerusalem to celebrate Passover. They had met with Him periodically whenever He was in Jerusalem. Such visits were never with His followers, always alone or with one of His close associates, John. They were concerned about the safety of Jesus in Jerusalem. When He entered Jerusalem with His throng of followers, He would emerge as an immediate threat to the power and influence of the Chief Priest. That was the topic of their discussion as they walked together.

It was close to sundown, the eve of the Sabbath. There was just enough time for them to reach their homes by sundown. Nicodemus and Joseph of Arimathea had just come from a meeting of the Sanhedrin which had been long and bitter. The subject had been Jesus.

The meeting had started off reasonably enough with discussion of current matters associated with the preparations for the Passover. It was midway in the discussion when Caiaphas interjected that he had heard rumors that Jesus was going to enter Jerusalem and spend the Passover, quite likely preaching to the people. Caiaphas seemed quite disturbed over the prospect. Annas supported him in voicing concern over the disruptive influence that Jesus would have upon the people. As they continued in the mutual reinforcement of their concerns, both became quite strong in their denunciation of Jesus as a threat to the civil order. As such, if the Romans were to become involved, there would be no limit to the repercussions of their displeasure. Unless this threat could be directed solely at

Jesus, there was some concern over continued amicable relations of the Temple with the Roman authorities.

Nicodemus and Joseph actually interpreted this as a concern on the part of Caiaphas and Annas of how their positions would be effected by Roman displeasure. They were now alert to a plot on the part of Caiaphas and Annas to associate any unrest or difficulty on the person of Jesus. In fact, they started discussing how they might eliminate the threat. It was Caiaphas who made the statement that one man's life was not worth the risk of creating public disorder. In other words, he was leaning more and more to the total elimination of Jesus, even to His execution.

Joseph of Arimathea had spoken up quite strongly against this idea, indicating that Jesus had a wide following and any attempt to silence Him or dispose of Him would create even more disorder because of the tremendous good that He had accomplished. Nicodemus also spoke up and said that it would be very difficult to execute Jesus in any set of circumstances because He was innocent of any crime, and He had a significant number of followers, many of whom would be in Jerusalem at that time.

In a very sly manner, Caiaphas suggested that it would be possible to separate Jesus from His followers, and even to hide from the Romans the fact that Jesus had a great following.

Joseph and Nicodemus did what they could to calm the waters, supported, to some extent, by other members of the Sanhedrin. By and large, however, the Sanhedrin remained neutral despite every attempt of Caiaphas and Annas to enlist them in an attempt to silence Jesus once and for all. Joseph and Nicodemus had left the meeting perturbed and continued their discussion as they travelled homeward.

"I believe the Chief Priest is unduly afraid of the influence of Jesus," said Joseph. "He seems to linger too much on trying to disprove the validity of the miracles that Jesus has performed."

"You are right," said Nicodemus. "Caiaphas spends an inordinate amount of time trying to vilify everything that Jesus has done and said. You and I have seen with our own eyes, and heard with our own ears, the impact for good that Jesus has had on the people in Judea. And now, if I can understand the rumors, He intends to come to Jerusalem next week."

"Why next week?" asked Joseph.

"I imagine it's because Jerusalem will be full of so many people from throughout Judea. The people of Jerusalem do not know Jesus. But the people in the countryside know Him well. Many will be here in preparation for Passover at the end of next week. I imagine that is one reason that Jesus is coming. Another would be the fact that He has never been here before on His ministry of preaching to the people, curing the sick, and even raising the dead."

Joseph shook his head a little. He seemed troubled. "I am concerned, my good friend. The Chief Priest is not going to take kindly to any kind of adulation received by Jesus. Caiaphas is a dangerous man; he will do anything to maintain his position and his power."

They walked on a short distance.

"Well he's afraid of both the Jews and the Romans," said Nicodemus. "That's quite a difficult position. He owes his position to the Romans who appointed him, and who expect him to keep the Jewish population under control. The Romans will be ruthless if there is any measure of disturbance. They will think nothing of crucifying hundreds of people, and deposing, if not even executing Caiaphas. In the Roman eyes, his title and appointment is one that suits their current policy. The Roman Procurator, Pontius Pilate, will support Caiaphas only so long as Caiaphas can control the Jewish people. Caiaphas sees Jesus as a threat to that control. We both know that is not true. Jesus preaches repentance and forgiveness. His message is spiritual. He sees His Kingdom as not of this world."

"Quite so," said Joseph. After a short pause he added, "How do you see that unfolding?"

"Well Jesus has created quite a following throughout Galilee and the countryside. He has spent a lot of time in the various towns, has cured many people of their ailments. These cures are real. You can't take a man who was blind from birth, who suddenly can see, and claim that it has been faked, as Caiaphas does. Only a short time ago He raised His friend Lazarus from the dead."

"What happened there, Joseph? I know the basic story but not all the facts."

Joseph related the story. Jesus had been away from Bethany where His good friend Lazarus lived with his sisters, Martha and Mary Magdalene. He visited them often. Lazarus became deathly ill, so the sisters sent word to Jesus, asking Him to come cure Lazarus. Lazarus died, and was buried for four days before Jesus arrived at their home. When He did arrive, He immediately went to the tomb and shouted, 'Lazarus, come out!' Within minutes, the stone in front of the tomb rolled aside, and Lazarus walked out. His burial bandages about him were stained but when they fell from around him, his body was whole. There was great amazement throughout the area as word spread that Jesus had raised Lazarus from the dead.

Nicodemus sighed, "That is a remarkable story, Joseph. I had heard talk of the miracle but I was not aware of the details. Thank you."

They walked on, deep in thought. Nicodemus continued, "Raising people from the dead cannot be faked. Didn't Jesus also raise a boy in Naim, and a daughter of Jarius, the leader of the Synagogue in Capernaum?"

"Yes, He did," assented Joseph. "With His miracles, and with His preaching of the need for repentance, Jesus is attracting many thoughtful people."

"But He is not convincing Caiaphas," added Nicodemus, "and He is alienating the Sadducees. The Sadducees, with Caiaphas as their leader, feel especially threatened because the preaching of Jesus runs totally counter to their faith. When Jesus preaches of the Kingdom to come, it contradicts their belief that there is no afterlife and everything ends with death."

"Yes," said Joseph. "As Pharisees, we believe in an afterlife, which is in concert with the preaching of Jesus. But even then, there are many of our fellow Pharisees who have attacked Jesus. If you will recall, Nicodemus, it was our fellow Pharisees who probed by presenting the coins to Him as to whether they should obey Caesar or God, to which Jesus replied 'Render unto Caesar that which is Caesar's and unto God that which is God's'".

"Do you see a serious threat to Jesus if He were to come into Jerusalem?" Nicodemus asked after further thought.

"Yes I do," said Joseph. "I would go so far as to say that Caiaphas might even make an attempt to have Jesus murdered while He is here."

Nicodemus shook his head. "Why can't that man just sit and listen? Jesus is no threat to the civil order. He is a threat only to those who turn their back on God. Jesus is continuing the work that was begun by John the Baptist."

Joseph gave a grunt. "And look what happened to John the Baptist. Herod had him beheaded because he was a threat to the status quo. Jesus, too, is now seen as a threat to the status quo. I am sure that when He enters Jerusalem next week, His followers who are in town will show great enthusiasm. I am certain that we will be called into a special meeting of the Sanhedrin to consider how to control the enthusiasm and support for Jesus."

The two walked on for a short distance, both deep in thought until they arrived at the home of Nicodemus. They spent a moment or two talking and then Joseph continued on to his own home. Both men remained firm in their concern for the safety of Jesus. Caiaphas was a treacherous man. He would destroy anything that was a threat to his power and position.

Chapter Two
The Search for a Traitor

Even as the two friends parted for the night, a meeting was taking place in the Temple. Caiaphas, the Chief Priest, was in a heated, at least for him, conversation with Annas. Annas served as the Priest in charge of finances in the Temple. He regulated the sale of merchandise for sacrifice, as well as the conversion of normal coins into the only coins used in the Temple, called the Tyre, valued at approximately half a Shekel. This created the opportunity for money-changers to compete and make a profit on each transaction. Since only Tyres could be used to purchase merchandise for sacrifice, this too created an opportunity for profit.

Caiaphas was in a rage. The meeting with the Sanhedrin had been inconclusive. He had not found the support he sought to eliminate the influence of Jesus. He had decided to proceed, find a way to have Jesus arrested, and then bring Him to trial before the Sanhedrin. He would control the trial so he could be sure of the outcome. Jesus had to be stopped. He would do it.

He paced angrily and excitedly up-and-down in front of Annas, who was seated and silent. "Rumors are that Jesus is coming to Jerusalem for the Passover celebration. He will probably use the opportunity to preach. He will have a large audience, since so many of His disciples from His travels in Galilee will also be here. Those crowds will attract many of the visitors and residents of Jerusalem who have not heard Him before.

He will use the opportunity to enlarge the number of His followers."

He paced rapidly and then abruptly stopped. He walked slowly over to where Annas was seated and looking directly at him stated firmly, "He must be stopped!"

Almost gritting his teeth, Caiaphas continued. "He is a threat to us and to the civil order."

Quietly Annas spoke up, "Calm yourself, Caiaphas. We must approach this carefully. As you say, Jesus is surrounded by His followers. Somehow or other we must find an opportunity when He is separated from His followers. Only then can we arrest Him. When He is in our hands, we can engineer the trial to find Him guilty of whatever we wish, and have Him executed. That will get rid of Him once and for all."

Annas' words calmed Caiaphas. In a more normal voice and relaxed demeanor he said, "Your counsel is wise, Annas. How do you suggest we find Him alone?"

"Everyone is alone sometime," said Annas. "We just have to find the opportunity." He continued, "This coming week, when He comes to Jerusalem, it should give us sufficient opportunity to arrest Him." He remained silent in deep thought for a moment. Then he added, "He will undoubtedly celebrate a Seder dinner. If He is true to form, He will do this with a limited number of His followers. That would be a perfect time to arrest Him."

"And how do we find where He is celebrating the Seder dinner?" asked Caiaphas.

With a mirthless grunt Annas replied, "A traitor will tell us."

A slow smile spread across the face of Caiaphas. "Of course! That is brilliant, Annas."

They both lapsed into deep thought.

Caiaphas had, for some time, been convinced that it was necessary to find someone who would betray Jesus. After careful thought, in consultation with priests of the Temple and the Temple guards, Caiaphas ascertained that the most logical candidate would be one Judas Iscariot. He seemed to be the money man of the followers of Jesus. He had been heard to voice criticism of Jesus as being an impractical dreamer, totally oblivious of the need to have money to buy things such as food. He also seemed to always be apart from the close followers of Jesus. In the opinion of those he asked, Judas was a loner who seemed to be on the fence with regard to his support for Jesus. As such he would be more prone to be interested in a payment for betraying Jesus.

"We know we have the person; how do we go about making a secret arrangement with him?" asked Caiaphas.

Annas laughed. "Caiaphas, my son, I'm surprised at how dense you can be at times. It's a very simple matter. Just have one of your guards indicate to Judas, quietly, when he is separated from his friends, which can easily be arranged, that you wish to see him. No reason is to be advanced. Judas is certainly wily enough to know that a meeting with you is not going to be a discussion on some point of scripture."

Caiaphas smiled. Addressing Annas in a formal manner he said "Sire, I am never surprised at how simple yet far-reaching your stratagems are." Caiaphas laughed derisively. "You are right! Asking Judas to meet with me is a stroke of genius. If he comes, then we know he is ours. If he ignores it, then we will have to look elsewhere. He will know that we do not wish to discuss scripture. So if he comes, as you say, he's in the bag!"

They both laughed.

Caiaphas called in the temple guard and told him to engineer an encounter with Judas. Judas was then to be invited to meet with Caiaphas.

Unknown to Caiaphas and Annas, Judas was becoming more and more concerned about the impractical nature of Jesus. In fact, Judas was more that perturbed, he was angry. It was left to him to handle the finances and to be able to meet any payment requirement. The pressure upon him to continually produce had reached the breaking point. He well understood the power of Jesus. He began to wonder how he could profit from his information about Jesus and His whereabouts. The enemies of Jesus would surely pay a reward for putting Jesus in their hands. He knew that if an attempt was made to arrest Him, with the flick of His finger He could overcome all of the guards instantaneously. Judas had seen many miracles performed by Jesus, including the raising from the dead of three persons. He was well aware of the power that Jesus had. As he pondered the dual situation of unlimited power on the part of Jesus, and the necessity for him to continually raise money, he decided that he might be able to arrive at an arrangement with the high priests where he could trade information in exchange for silver. That would be found money since there was no way that the Temple authorities would be able to truly arrest and detain Jesus. Judas smiled, his thoughts full of anticipation.

Chapter Three
Fulfillment of the Covenant

The next morning the two friends met again and walked together to the Temple to observe the Sabbath. Their conversation continued in the same vein. As they walked, they noticed that there were many strangers in the city. The city was crowded. Many had come in preparation for the Passover festivities which would begin towards the end of the week.

As they returned to their homes later in the day, they continued in their discussion. As they parted at the home of Nicodemus, Joseph said, "Tomorrow starts another week. I hope that Jesus does not come to Jerusalem. I am afraid that Caiaphas will scheme and plan to do Him great harm." After a short pause he added, "He might even try to execute Him. That would be a terrible miscarriage of justice. Jesus has committed no crime!"

"Nicodemus, my friend, you have heard Caiaphas on more than one occasion say, 'The life of one man is not as important as the salvation of the nation.' He equates his position, his influence, and even his power and income, as being the nation. What foolishness! He is the Chief Priest at the beck-and-call of the Roman authorities. With the flick of an eyelash he could be removed, and even executed. He knows that. He knows that he must continue to please the Roman authorities. Hence, anything that causes them disquiet is a serious problem for him. That is why he fears Jesus."

"But perhaps, Joseph, there is another factor here. John the Baptist preached that redemption was possible without sacrifice, merely by repentance. That message strikes directly at the heart of the Temple. Our belief is one of sacrifice. Our prayers and supplications arise out of the fear of retribution for our misdeeds. John the Baptist, and now Jesus, have interjected a God of love, a God who accepts our repentance and forgives our sins. Sacrifice is not required. This is a threat to the reason for the very existence of the Temple. Without the need for sacrifice to appease a God whom we fear, there is no need for a place where sacrifice is performed."

Nicodemus was startled with this comment. As they walked on, he pondered the point. Suddenly began to see the threat that Jesus must be to Caiaphas and to the Temple authorities. This sense of threat was certainly not improved with Jesus' comment that the Temple would be destroyed and in three days He would recreate it. What did He mean by this? The entire history of the teaching of Jesus was one of love -- love of God, love of neighbor, and more importantly, the love of God for His creatures. The idea of a vengeful God being assuaged by sacrifice was replaced by a loving God welcoming with open arms a repentant sinner.

Nicodemus smiled broadly as the thought took hold. Now he began to understand more clearly many of his conversations with Jesus.

They stopped as they arrived at the Temple. "Joseph," said Nicodemus, "we must continue our discussion on our way back later. I have a story to tell you."

With that, they entered the Temple.

After the Sabbath services they left the Temple to walk together back to their residences.

Nicodemus picked up where he had left off on the way to the Temple.

"Joseph, the point you have made is very important. It not only has clarified in my mind why Caiaphas feels so threatened, but more important, it has clarified many of the teachings of Jesus. The parable He tells of the prodigal son summarizes, to a large extent, the essence of His teaching. The father will always forgive, with joy in his heart, the sins of any son who repents and begs forgiveness." Joseph asks, "What is the story?"

Nicodemus said, 'There was a man who had two sons. The younger son said, "Father, give me the share of the property that will belong to me." The father then divided his property. A few days later the younger son gathered all that his father had given him, travelled to a distant country, and squandered his inheritance in dissolute living. When he had spent everything, a severe famine took place throughout that country, and he began to be in need. He was forced to hire himself out to one of the citizens of that country, who sent him to work in his fields. He would have gladly filled himself with the feed that the pigs were eating; but no one gave him anything. But he came to a realization and said, "How many of my father's hired hands have bread enough to spare, but here I am dying of hunger! I will go to my father, and I will say to him, 'Father, I have sinned against Heaven and before you; I am no longer worthy to be called your son; I beg of you to treat me like one of your hired hands.'" So he set off on his journey to the home of his father and the lands that he would have owned. But while he was still far off, his father saw him and was filled with compassion; he ran and put his arms around his youngest son and kissed him. The son then said to him, "Father, I have sinned against Heaven and before you; I am no longer worthy to be called your son." But the father said to his slaves, "Quickly, bring out a robe - the best one - and put it on him; put a ring on his finger and sandals on his feet. Get the fatted calf and kill it, and let us eat and celebrate; for this son of mine was dead and is alive again; he was lost and is found!" And they began to celebrate.

The elder son was in the field during the arrival of his younger brother; and when he approached the house, he heard music and dancing. He called to a slave and asked what was going on. He replied, "Your brother has returned, and your father has killed the fatted calf in celebration, because he has got him back safe and sound." The older brother became angry and refused to go in. His father came out and began to plead with him. He answered his father, "Listen! For all of these years I have been working like a slave for you, and I have never disobeyed your command; yet you have never given me even a young goat so that I might celebrate with my friends. But when this son of yours comes back, who has squandered your property with prostitutes, you kill the fatted calf for him!" Then the father said to him, "Son, you are always with me, and all that is mine is yours, but we had to celebrate and rejoice, because this brother of yours was dead and has come to life; he was lost and has been found.'"

With that they walked on, and after a short distance arrived at the home of Joseph. As they had walked that short distance Joseph had remained silent in deep contemplation.

As they were about to part, Joseph looked directly at Nicodemus, made eye contact, and said quietly, "I see.

Jesus is the fulfillment of the law. We live under a code of fear of the all-powerful God. We offer sacrifice in appeasement and supplication. We offer sacrifice for the forgiveness of our sins. John the Baptist came along and preached remorse and repentance. He was beheaded. Now Jesus comes forth and preaches beyond John the Baptist. He preaches forgiveness almost for the asking. The only requirement is remorse for sins, and the will to sin no more. Jesus preaches the love of God for us and the love of us for God." Joseph paused and looked meaningfully at Nicodemus, who silently nodded.

"Yes," he said. "Jesus is truly fulfillment of the preaching the Covenant God made with Adam. Jesus is truly from God.

Joseph sighed. He seemed to grow as if the thought he felt in his mind was swelling his whole being. "If not part of God."

With that he turned and entered his home.

ROCCO LEONARD MARTINO

Chapter Four
The Entry into Jerusalem

Jesus had stayed in Bethany first at the house of Simon the Leper, and then at the home of His good friend Lazarus.

It had been a long day. Jesus and His followers had travelled from Capernaum to Bethany to spend the Sabbath and a few days with Lazarus, Martha, and Mary. Jesus was weary, but still exuberant, buoyed at all times by the reflected joy of those He cured and influenced as He travelled.

First, however, He had promised to have dinner at the home of Simon.

Simon was a Pharisee whom Jesus had cured of leprosy. As they reclined at table, engaged in a spirited conversation, a woman of the community known to Simon and to Jesus entered carrying an alabaster flask full of ointment. Weeping, and standing behind Him, she began to bathe the feet of Jesus with her tears, and then to wipe them with her hair. Then she anointed Him with the ointment from the alabaster jar.

Simon was perturbed, if not enraged. "Woman, you are a sinner. How dare you enter my home? How dare you waste such precious oil by using it to anoint the feet of my guest? Be gone!"

The woman was shocked. Jesus looked up in surprise, and smiled.

"Simon, I have something to say to you."

Somewhat mollified, Simon asked "What is it, Teacher?"

Jesus began to tell him a story. He said, "Two men were in debt to a moneylender. One owed him 500 denarii, and the other 50. When they couldn't pay it back, he generously canceled the debts for both of them. Now which of them will love him more?"

Simon answered, "I suppose the one who had the larger debt canceled."

Jesus told him, "You have answered correctly."

Then, turning to the woman, He told Simon, "Do you see this woman? I came into your house, Simon. You didn't give me any water for my feet, but this woman has washed my feet with her tears and dried them with her hair. You didn't give me a kiss, but this woman, from the moment I came in, has not stopped kissing my feet. You didn't anoint my head with oil, but this woman has anointed my feet with perfume. So I say to you that her sins, as many as they are, have been forgiven, and that's why she has shown such great love. But the one to whom little is forgiven loves little."

Then Jesus told her, "Your sins are forgiven!"

Those who were at the table with them began to say among themselves, "Who is this man who even forgives sins?"

But Jesus told the woman, "Your faith has saved you. Go in peace."

Simon was taken aback. A very thoughtful man, he suddenly realized how fortunate he had been to have Jesus cure him. He turned to Jesus and begged His forgiveness for his bad manners.

Jesus smiled. Then He added "And you too, Simon, may go in peace."

The next day, the eve of the Sabbath, Jesus sat quietly with His friends Lazarus, Martha, and Mary Magdalene.

Throughout dinner and afterwards they discussed His trip to Jerusalem following the Sabbath. It would be the first day of the week prior to the Passover celebration. Jerusalem would be full of people coming from all parts of Judea to celebrate. Jesus thought it would be a great opportunity for Him to enter Jerusalem because many of His followers around Judea would also be in Jerusalem. Since He began His ministry, He had not visited Jerusalem with His followers, although He had visited alone, or with John, on various occasions.

Lazarus pointed out that while this would be an advantage for Jesus to visit Jerusalem now, it could be a disadvantage because of the hubbub and turmoil with so many visitors. In addition, the Chief Priest, Caiaphas, would certainly try to use the occasion to do Him harm.

Jesus smiled; turmoil had been a constant companion throughout His travels.

"But Jesus," said Lazarus, "you don't know how treacherous these people can be."

Jesus smiled. "But I do!" Jesus paused and looked in a sad and meaningful way at Lazarus. "You must know that I expect to be betrayed and executed in Jerusalem."

Lazarus was shocked. He had heard Jesus before speak of His betrayal and execution, and he had received reports from the other apostles who had heard of Jesus' prophecy of His own death in the same fashion. He also knew that Jesus had prophesied that at the end of the third day He would rise from the dead. His words were that the Temple would be destroyed and in three days it would be rebuilt. He was referring to Himself as the Temple.

He knew that Jesus had tremendous power. He had seen Jesus cure many, and he, Lazarus, had actually been brought back to life after being in his grave for four days. The fact that Jesus was prophesying His own death and resurrection from the dead did not surprise him, but it did dismay him.

"Jesus, as a friend, can you not have this cup pass from you? Is it necessary for you to go to Jerusalem even at the risk of your life?"

Jesus once again smiled quietly. "My good friend, Lazarus," He began, "It is necessary. The prophecy must be fulfilled."

"But, Jesus, surely there must be another way."

It was Jesus who suddenly decided to change the topic. With a broad smile He looked directly at Lazarus and began, "Passover is a time of great joy. We must all celebrate the occasion. Be of good cheer, Lazarus. Let us have a quiet dinner together and not dwell further upon any difficulty in the future."

With that, Jesus maintained a conversation full of joy for Lazarus and his two sisters.

When asked where He would stay, He mentioned His good friends Nicodemus and Joseph of Arimathea. On the other hand, He thought it best to simply return each day to Bethany.

Lazarus was enthusiastic about this possibility. "This is your home, Jesus. Please always think of it as such."

Jesus and His friends talked long into the night, reminiscing at length over so many happy times, especially the raising of Lazarus from the dead. Lazarus in turn was happy to be in company with His good friend Jesus, and looking forward to being with Him and the apostles in Jerusalem for Passover.

They celebrated the Sabbath together in prayer.

THE CROSS OF VICTORY

The next morning, on the first day of the week, they set out for Jerusalem. As they proceeded, they were joined by more and more people heading towards Jerusalem as well. Many had been cured by Jesus of their afflictions over many years. Soon the procession took on a very festive and joyous mood. Some cut palm fronds and small trees and waved them. The mood continued to lift and soon singing broke out. This in turn attracted more marchers to join the group. It swelled until it became a parade.

In the usual fashion, in a happy occasion like this, there was much discussion as well as singing. Soon the singing took precedence, and as they travelled their happy voices raised in song carried to the gates of Jerusalem.

There were many who were travelling to Jerusalem on this day. They were attracted by this cortège accompanying Jesus and soon the crowd swelled.

Before setting out, Jesus had instructed one of His followers to proceed into the town and to find a white colt and to bring it to Him.

Later, in the midst of their march to Jerusalem, when the colt was brought to Him, Jesus mounted it, and rode the colt, in the midst of the procession. As they neared the gates of Jerusalem, there were some who threw cloaks on the ground so that Jesus and the colt walked over them. This intensified as they entered the gates of Jerusalem and proceeded to the Temple square.

Chapter Five
Jesus, a Threat to the Civil Order

Inhabitants and tourists in the city heard the procession before they saw it. It was mid-morning on the first day of the week. There was a great bustle in Jerusalem, with the tourists from the rest of the country milling about. There seemed an air of expectation. In the distance cries were heard. There seemed to be a large group of people approaching the gates of the city. The inhabitants, and the visitors, looked towards the gates wondering what the commotion was. What they saw was a tall figure riding a white colt in front of a large group of followers. All of them were singing, and some were waving palm fronds. As the crowd approached the gates, the word "Jesus" could be heard continually repeated in a cadence. Those who knew immediately recognized that the lead figure in the group was Jesus, the carpenter from Nazareth. The cadence of His name called time and time again by those following was suddenly picked up by those in the city who knew Him and they too began to sing His praises. "Jesus, Jesus, Son of David, Hosanna in the highest." As He came through the main square, many threw flowers before Him, and great cheers followed Him as He proceeded through the city.

The Roman guards stood aside to let Jesus proceed on His way. They were impressed by the adulation of the people who followed Him into the city, and those who were in the city that seemed to know Him. The Roman soldiers recognized that this was a peaceful tribute to a favorite and not something that they should be concerned about stopping.

Caiaphas, on the other hand, saw the adulation as he was walking through the main square. He was appalled. Tentacles of fear gripped his heart. Jesus seemed to have tremendous support amongst the common people. In fact, Caiaphas mused, His support seemed even stronger than that for himself. If Jesus were to attack his position, Caiaphas would be in trouble. All of his foreboding seemed to overwhelm him. He walked briskly to the Temple to his quarters and pondered for a long period of time what action he could and must take to counter the apparent strong influence of Jesus upon the people.

He decided on an immediate meeting of the Sanhedrin and issued instructions to the guards for such a meeting in the late afternoon.

He was surprised that so many members of the Sanhedrin were able to attend. As they all assembled, they seemed a little surprised and wondered why the meeting had been called after such a short period of time following the long meeting on the eve of the Sabbath. That was only two days ago.

Caiaphas entered. He briskly strode to the front of the room, turned and addressed the gathering. "Members of the Sanhedrin." The murmurs ceased and a hush came over the room as everyone looked towards Caiaphas in expectation of an explanation for the meeting.

"I do not have to describe what occurred today. The carpenter of Nazareth, Jesus bar Joseph, entered the city. It had all the appearances of a triumphant procession." These last words Caiaphas uttered as if he was virtually spitting them out. It was obvious that he was upset and angry. He continued.

"This Jesus is a threat to the civil order. We..."

Joseph of Arimathea interrupted Caiaphas. "How so, Caiaphas? In what sense is He a threat to the public order? I, too, saw His entry into Jerusalem and from my perspective I saw respect and adulation, if not love, for someone who has done so much for so many people. We all know, including you, Caiaphas that Jesus has cured many people of their illness, has raised the dead, and has preached repentance and forgiveness. He is certainly no threat to the civil order. If anything, He is a promoter of civil order."

Caiaphas was stunned. He knew that he did not have the support of Joseph of Arimathea, Nicodemus, and many other Pharisees. He ruled the Sanhedrin because of the numerical superiority of the Sadducees, his group. He did not shirk this battle. He had to win it!

In a thunderous voice, Caiaphas virtually shouted, "You are wrong, Joseph. He is a threat. Let me tell you how."

Joseph decided not to interrupt but to give Caiaphas an opportunity to vent before he would deflate his comments.

"Jesus speaks of His Kingdom," said Caiaphas. "He represents Himself as King of the Jews." There was a murmur in the room. There were many who agreed because of the remarks attributed to Jesus that had been reported to members of the Sanhedrin. Caiaphas continued, "He seeks to gain the support of innumerable people by purporting to be a wizard who cures them of their illness. It is all trickery. With regard to the famous instance of having His friend raised from the dead, that is more trickery. Lazarus could have stayed in the tomb until Jesus came by and said 'come out' and he came out.

It's all trickery. No human has the power to raise others from the dead".

Joseph gave a loud laugh. It startled Caiaphas. Joseph said, "And if a man is blind from birth and can see, how can that be trickery? And if a man is paralyzed, from birth, and has no use of his legs, and suddenly can get up and walk, then how is that trickery? And if a body stinketh after being in a tomb for four days and can come out alive, how is that trickery?"

Joseph took a deep breath then continued. "You are wrong Caiaphas," said Joseph. "Jesus is a true miracle worker. He seems to be anointed by God. He is special. We would be better off listening to Him than attacking Him."

"I see that I am wasting my time trying to convince you, Joseph. Perhaps you will agree with me that the civil order is important. Will you agree with that Joseph?"

Joseph remained silent for a moment. The question was innocuous and obvious. But there had to be a trick in it or Caiaphas would not have posed it. Carefully and slowly he answered. "Yes," said Joseph. "Of course I will agree to that."

"Will you agree that we must maintain the civil order or the Romans will do it in a more brutal fashion?"

Once again, slowly and reluctantly, Joseph answered. "Yes, of course I will agree to that, Caiaphas".

"Then will you agree that the need for the preservation of the civil order is more important than the life of one man, no matter who that is, including me?" said Caiaphas.

Joseph laughed. He was joined by Nicodemus and a number of others around the room. In a mirthful way Joseph said, "Frankly, Caiaphas, I can't see you as a threat to the civil order." Casting a quizzical eye towards Caiaphas, Joseph added, "But I do see you trying to destroy anybody who stands in your way, or who interferes with your power base. Is that not so Caiaphas?" Caiaphas was a little startled but not angered. He laughed.

"Joseph, my good friend, anyone would be concerned of threats to their position and influence. You, too, I am certain. Even if you don't admit it, all of us know it would be true. You're doing that now. You disagree with me so you are attacking whatever I say. You see this as a threat to your opinions. While it might annoy me, it has not angered me because I understand it. But, Joseph, will you not agree that the public order is more important than the life of one man, no matter who that man may be? If Jesus becomes a threat to the public order, and we agree to that, then He must be removed, one way or another. Will you agree to that?"

"No!" thundered Joseph. He was joined by an equal thundering, "No!" from Nicodemus. "Jesus can never be a threat. Use some other name such as Barabbas. Barabbas is a threat, and he is now incarcerated and should be executed. We can all agree to that. He is a threat to the public order."

Caiaphas laughed. "Alright. We won't use Jesus as the example but we will say that anyone who is a threat to the public order should be removed, if not executed. Can we agree to that?"

Reluctantly, Joseph said, "Yes".

"Then we can proceed and keep a watchful eye on everything that happens this week and if anyone in addition to Barabbas is a threat to the civil order, then that person must be apprehended and brought to the attention of the Roman authorities. Can we all agree on that?"

Both Joseph of Arimathea and Nicodemus looked at each other; somewhere in these words there was a trick about which they were concerned. But the logic was not something they could dispute. Reluctantly, they agreed.

The Sanhedrin was unanimous in supporting Caiaphas on the position that the public order was more important than the life of one man. If anyone threatened the public order then certainly that person should be brought to the attention of the Roman authorities.

As everyone left the room, Caiaphas could not help but feel elated. He had succeeded in planting the seed that the public order was more important than the life of one man. All he had to do now was prove that Jesus was a threat to the public order or a threat to the stability of the Jewish religion. In doing that, he would be able to show that Jesus was a threat to the public order as a threat to the observance of the Jewish religion. Best of all if he could maneuver Jesus into a blasphemy, this would be automatic condemnation that no one, including Joseph and Nicodemus, would be able to dispute.

Caiaphas remained in deep thought for a considerable period of time. How could he control Jesus? He decided to discuss this with Annas. He asked the guard to invite Annas to meet with him.

When Annas came, Caiaphas explained to him his concerns about the impact of Jesus upon the status quo. Annas was very direct. "Why don't you have Him followed and have reports at all times as to what He is doing? In this fashion you will be able to do two things at the same time. If the follower is smart enough to be a heckler as well, then perhaps he can discredit Jesus before the people of Jerusalem. At the same time you will be able to accumulate evidence that you can use in bringing Jesus to trial."

"I like your idea of a trial," said Caiaphas. "That is my objective as well. I would especially like to find evidence to prove that Jesus blasphemed so that we can condemn Him to death. I am convinced that He must be removed. If He is not, then He will continue in His popularity with the people and pose a significant threat to our authority." Caiaphas paused and then continued. "We must find a way to arrest Him. Then we can stage a trial that we can control completely and have Him sentenced to death."

Annas nodded in agreement. "Yes," he said. "A good plan. But His popularity is a problem." Annas paused in thought and then continued. "You will have to get Him away from His followers or you will never be able to arrest Him without causing a major disturbance. We cannot afford any disturbance or the Romans will become involved, and that will be difficult for us. They will accuse us of being unable to maintain order. We cannot afford that!"

"Then we must arrest Him when He is alone" said Caiaphas.

"Easier said than done," retorted Annas.

The two men continued their discussion for some time. The problem of separating Jesus from His followers was not resolved. Hopefully, Judas would agree to betray Jesus so He could be arrested.

Additional information on the activities of Jesus was essential. The end result was that Caiaphas dispatched Temple guards in street clothes to follow Jesus and to report back on His activities. In addition, he dispatched his most senior and trusted Temple priest, also in street clothes, with instructions to disrupt, to the extent possible, any meeting of Jesus with the people of Jerusalem. Finally, he dispatched another guard in street clothes to search for Judas, again with an invitation to meet with Caiaphas.

Still pondering the issue of separating Jesus from His followers, Annas left.

Caiaphas was finally satisfied that he was doing everything possible to thwart Jesus, moving towards His execution. The only fly in the ointment was the popularity of Jesus with the people. He would have to find a way to separate Jesus from His supporters and have Him executed before the people found out. Caiaphas sighed. This Jesus was certainly trouble. But at least He was now close to being in his grasp and under his power.

As he proceeded to dinner with his family, he smiled. The thought raced through his mind. "At last he would have Jesus in his power!"

Chapter Six
Jesus in the Temple

The new day dawned bright but chilly. It was early Spring and the air had a crispness and a delightful smell that invigorated the spirit. It was typical of a Spring morning in Jerusalem, elevated above the desert and plains all around. There was a stir in the city as Jesus entered the gate. The walk from Bethany and the home of Lazarus had been leisurely and bracing. Once through the gate, He proceeded to the Temple.

He was accompanied by His apostles, Peter and John. They had spent an agreeable evening and night at the home of Lazarus whose hospitality was without bounds when it came to Jesus.

As they approached the Temple, the din increased significantly. In the days preceding the Passover celebration, there were many who were proceeding to the Temple for their offerings to expiate their sins or to praise God. Knowing of this annual influx of such offerings, the Temple authorities had increased the supply of doves and lambs, and the money-changers had significantly increased the coins, called Tyres, which had to be used for any transaction associated with Temple offerings. The money-changers always showed a considerable profit. As a matter of fact, their activity during this particular week was a major factor in their annual income. The Temple authorities also participated in this profit as they facilitated the arrangements that allowed the money-changers to function in the Temple. The Temple authorities also received some profit from the sale of lambs which were sacrificed by the Priests of the Temple. The sale of doves also brought considerable profit.

Annas, a prior Chief Priest, profited significantly as well. Despite being deposed of his title almost twenty years ago, he still exercised great power, having engineered the appointment of his five sons as Chief Priest, and now having his son-in-law Caiaphas chosen by the Procurator Pontius Pilate to be the Chief Priest. To say the least, Annas was the power behind the throne.

Caiaphas had risen early to supervise the activities in the Temple at the start of this week of preparation prior to the Passover celebration. As he walked through the Temple portico he smiled broadly as he viewed the activity. His smiled turned to a scowl as he saw Jesus walking towards the Temple. He stopped, wondering why Jesus was coming to the Temple. Then he realized that this was the normal procedure for Jesus to visit the Synagogue of whatever town He was in. Caiaphas suddenly realized that Jesus was now visiting the Temple just as He would visit the Synagogue.

He decided not to make a scene in trying to sway Jesus from entering the Temple. There was no basis for him to do such a thing. Still, he would have much preferred Jesus not to come to the Temple. Caiaphas turned his back on Jesus and went elsewhere in the Temple.

A short time later, the Temple guards had notified Caiaphas of a disturbance caused by Jesus. The details were scant. But Caiaphas was immediately concerned. Apparently Jesus had thrown over the tables of the money-changers. Caiaphas became furious. He immediately demanded to know where Jesus was. When told that Jesus had entered the Temple, Caiaphas immediately started to go after Jesus but then stopped abruptly. He thought very carefully over the circumstances and decided that Jesus had gone too far. Caiaphas walked slowly back to his meeting room in the Temple.

He pondered over the situation and decided that he had to immediately accelerate his move to eliminate Jesus. Jesus was now a threat not only to his power base but to his income. Jesus had to be stopped.

A short time later, an enraged Annas stormed in.

Annas was beside himself with rage. He stormed into the meeting room set aside for the Chief Priest, controlling his anger as he added further details for Caiaphas on what Jesus had done. Jesus had entered the area of the money-changers, woven a whip of some kind from leather thongs He carried, and proceeded to whip the money-changers and then to upset their tables, shouting at all times that they were desecrating His father's house. Then He turned to the animal merchants, released the pens, and flogged them as well, screaming too at them that they were desecrating His father's house. Then He entered the Temple and began disputing the readings with those gathered there.

Caiaphas was further aghast in surprise, and then became equally angry. While Annas was immediately affected since he was the financial beneficiary of the profit from the money-changers and the sale of the lambs, Caiaphas was concerned about threats to his power base. If the Romans became alarmed at such disturbances, they could very well replace him. He calmed his anxiety as he asked Annas, "Did He do anything else?" After a moment he added, "Did the Romans observe this?"

Annas calmed his anger as he spat out, "No, the Romans did not, but our people certainly did!"

Caiaphas understood. This act by Jesus was the throwing down of a gauntlet challenging Annas and Caiaphas in their authority and jurisdiction.

"I think He did great damage to us! He cost me weeks of profit when He upset the tables and the money-changers. There is no guarantee that all of the money that was on the tables has been recovered. In addition, many of the vendors of lambs became concerned and left." As an afterthought he added, "The doves have flown away and will never be recaptured." Annas went on and on, almost wailing at his profit loss. Suddenly Caiaphas laughed derisively.

"Annas you are sounding like a merchant instead of a Priest. You and I both know that your profit will be recovered since those who intend to sacrifice will indeed sacrifice. So the money-changers and animal merchants will suffer no real loss except for one of dignity. It is only a short delay factor. As far as coins that are lost in the Temple, I don't believe it. In the Temple people will bring the coins to you. If this were the market squares I would say that your losses would have been much larger. So stop your wailing. We have to plan our action to make sure that Jesus is stopped."

Annas abruptly stopped and paid close attention to what Caiaphas had said. Caiaphas continued, "We have to stop this man. This is the last straw in my mind. We have to get rid of Him now while we have the opportunity. We cannot allow Him to slip out of our fingers. Now let us think how we can do this."

THE CROSS OF VICTORY

The two remained in deep thought for a period of time. Very suddenly, Caiaphas looked up at Annas and said, "We have to arrest Him, try Him, and find Him guilty so that He can be executed. We have to do this quickly since we cannot be in the midst of a trial with Him through Passover, we have to do this now, before the Passover celebration. That does not give us much time. We have to arrest Him. As we discussed previously, the best way to do that is when He is separated from His followers, or preferably even alone. We have to arrest Him in the next two or three days. We have to execute Him before His followers have any idea of what we are doing. As we agreed, we need someone to betray Him. Is Judas still our candidate? Do you have any other ideas?"

"His disciples are very loyal to Him. As we already discussed, the only possible exception might be Judas Iscariot. We have even invited him to meet with you. He is a Zealot who seems to like money. He is the only immediate follower or apostle of Jesus who is not from Galilee. Remember, as we said before, he acts as their treasurer and is always complaining and moaning about the lack of the money that they have for their expenses. I am certain that he is pocketing some of the money for his own personal use, but I have no proof."

"Did you make attempts to approach him?"

"Of course. Hopefully, he may even intend to approach us this week. We have not seen him in Jerusalem before so we must work quickly to take advantage of this opportunity."

"With or without someone like Judas betraying Jesus, I intend to move forward to arrest Him this week. Pontius Pilate is due back in Jerusalem and I intend on seeing him and making the arrangements for an arresting troop made up of Roman soldiers as well as Temple guards. Such a move will show solidarity, and also enhance a successful arrest even if it is done when Jesus is surrounded by His followers. A show of great force by professional soldiers and guards can certainly overcome the opposition of untrained followers, no matter how strong their allegiance to Jesus."

Caiaphas paused for a moment and then looking again directly at Annas asked, "Do you agree?"

Annas nodded in assent, and very quietly left. Caiaphas paced a little and pondered and decided that his plan was sound. As soon as he determined that Pontius Pilate was in Jerusalem, he would make efforts to see him to finalize his plan of arrest.

The plan for arrest was now firm in the mind of Caiaphas. He would conclude the arrangements to have the Roman soldiers and the Temple guards ready to march at a moment's notice to arrest Jesus as soon as they knew He was relatively alone. If possible, they would bribe someone to betray such information about Jesus. Perhaps it could be that Judas Iscariot. But it had to be someone.

Jesus would undoubtedly be present at a first Seder dinner. That would be the time, immediately after when He would be virtually alone, to arrest Him. It now looked as if it would be on Thursday night (Yom Chamishi – the fifth day) close to the ninth hour.

Caiaphas walked back into the area where the money-changers were located. As he walked, he pondered who might betray Jesus if Judas did not respond.

Caiaphas paced back and forth, rapt in deep thought. Finally after a considerable amount of time he seemed to have come to a conclusion. He called for the Chief of the Temple guard. When he entered he instructed him to seek out Jesus, and His followers, and try and isolate Judas Iscariot. Did he know Judas Iscariot? The Chief of the Temple guard told Caiaphas that he did. Caiaphas then instructed him.

"Do not alarm him. Try and get him to come and see me without telling anyone about the meeting. Indicate or try to leave the impression that it will be a friendly meeting and he should have no fear. That should peak his curiosity enough to get him to come. When that happens, give me fair warning that he is coming and bring Judas to my home. Do you understand?"

"Yes, sire" said the guard.

Before the guard could leave to spread the word to all the Temple guards, Caiaphas added. "I have previously instructed Temple guards to seek Judas Iscariot and invite him to come and see me. Find these men and tell them that you alone will issue the invitation. Is that clear?"

"Yes, sire" the Chief guard said. "Be assured I will find Judas as you request."

With that, the Chief guard saluted and left.

Caiaphas continued his pacing for a few more moments before stopping and walking out of the room into the portico where he greeted the visitors to the Temple.

ROCCO LEONARD MARTINO

Chapter Seven
The Betrayal Plot

Later that day, as Caiaphas was reclining at dinner in his home, a Temple guard came with Judas Iscariot. He was escorted into the atrium where Caiaphas dismissed the guard and met with Judas alone.

With a broad smile, Caiaphas greeted Judas, "My good man, thank you for coming to see me. I have a matter of great importance to discuss with you and I would appreciate this opportunity to secure your opinion and hopefully your cooperation in a very important matter."

Judas was apprehensive. He was, of course, concerned at being summoned, no matter how discreetly, to meet with the Chief Priest. He knew that the Chief Priest was an enemy of Jesus. He was hoping that perhaps this enmity was mellowing and decreasing. Hence he had come and he would listen to what the Chief Priest had to say.

Caiaphas paced back and forth a number of times and then turned and with a smile once more addressed Judas.

"I wanted to see you because I need your cooperation. I want to bring Jesus here, or preferably to the Temple to meet with me and the Sanhedrin. I do not want this to be a major disturbance so that I am concerned at what the reaction would be if my guards were to summon Him and bring Him, with force if necessary, to meet with me. I would rather that the invitation to meet with me be done away from a crowd, and preferably when Jesus is all alone."

Judas was surprised, but not greatly. He suspected that Caiaphas wanted to arrest Jesus but was concerned that doing this in a crowded situation where there might be sufficient resistance as to mitigate or even make the arrest impossible. Caiaphas was concerned about the public order and also about the popularity of Jesus. Arresting Jesus would not be a clever move in a large crowd. Judas wondered, however, why Caiaphas would think that he would betray Jesus.

Caiaphas was all smiles. As if by telepathy he totally understood the thoughts in the mind of Judas. He decided to take the direct approach.

"My good man, I understand that you are the treasurer of Jesus and His band of followers. Is that not so?"

"Yes, that is so," said Judas.

"Then," continued Caiaphas, "I am prepared to pay you silver pieces if you can arrange to have my men approach Jesus with the invitation when He is alone or with a limited number of followers."

Ever the money man Judas said eagerly, "How many?"

Caiaphas decided not to bargain. He would make the bribe high enough to be successful. "Thirty pieces."

Greedily Judas asked, "How about fifty?"

Sternly Caiaphas quietly lashed out, "Thirty and stop being greedy."

Subdued, Judas bowed his head in deep thought.

Judas was stunned. Thirty pieces of silver was a considerable amount of money. He was interested in how he could acquire the money without betraying Jesus.

That seemed difficult. In a sense, he would be betraying Jesus by bringing the guards to Him when He was somewhat defenseless, but, Judas continued to reason, Jesus was powerful. He could call on His host of angels and demolish the guards with the wave of one finger. Judas smiled inwardly without giving Caiaphas any indication as to what he was thinking. As a matter of fact he decided to feign great anger.

In an angry voice, Judas said, "You insult me, Chief Priest. I am not a traitor and I am not willing to betray Jesus to you no matter how many pieces of silver you may dangle. Yes, of course, thirty pieces of silver does interest me. It would interest anyone. But the price is too low for what you are requesting."

Caiaphas laughed. "Don't be ridiculous, Judas. Jesus is a trickster. You are starting to believe that." As he said this Judas shook his head strongly. Caiaphas continued, "There is no point in shaking your head. You must realize that Jesus is a trickster. Otherwise He truly is from God. And if He is from God, no power on earth can arrest Him. So you see if He indeed is an honest man, He cannot be detained or arrested, and you can pocket thirty pieces of silver that is my loss. If, on the other hand, He is a trickster, and does not have the power to resist arrest, then you have not betrayed Jesus, but you have earned the gratitude of the Jewish people for exposing Him to be a fraud."

Judas was stunned. Of course Jesus was not a trickster. He had seen too many of the miracles of Jesus -- curing the sick and bringing the dead back to life. Inwardly, he smiled. Jesus would not allow Himself to be arrested. Judas would pocket the money and Caiaphas would not be able to arrest Jesus. Judas decided to remain silent for a period of time to keep Caiaphas in suspense as to what his reply would be.

Caiaphas, in turn, was absolutely convinced that the greed of Judas would lead him to betray Jesus. He, too, remained silent in expectation that Judas would attempt to ask for more silver, which he did.

"Thirty pieces of silver seems to be a small amount, Caiaphas. I still think it should be fifty."

"Then you have decided what to do and it is only a matter of price. Is that not so, Judas?"

Sheepishly, Judas looked directly at Caiaphas and very quietly said, "Yes".

Caiaphas had won. "Then my good man, it will be thirty pieces of silver and not one more. And if you continue to bargain with me I will reduce it to twenty."

Judas was beaten. In a quiet voice he asked, "And when will it be paid?"

"When Jesus is arrested. When He is brought to me, then I will have thirty pieces of silver dispatched to you. Is that agreed?"

Greedily Judas raised his voice slightly and strongly objected. "No! Payment must be made now."

Caiaphas laughed in derision. "No, Judas. Payment will be after you deliver Jesus into our hands. How else can I be sure you will keep your word?" Then looking directly at Judas, he added in a biting tone. "Your word, Judas!"

Morosely, looking towards Caiaphas, and mumbling in a low voice, Judas agreed.

They went on to discuss the further details as to how this was to be accomplished. Judas agreed to send word via one of the Temple guards to Caiaphas as to what would be the opportune time. Judas was not certain but at this time he believed that there was to be a dinner on the first day of Passover and immediately after the dinner Jesus would either be alone or be accompanied by very few of His followers. That seemed to be the opportune time. When this was determined and the location established, Judas would inform Caiaphas. It was further agreed that Judas would even come to Caiaphas and would lead the Temple guards to Jesus, and even kiss Him on the cheek to indicate which of the men at the meeting Jesus was.

The bargain was sealed, and Judas left, convinced that while it might appear that he was betraying Jesus, in reality he was really gaining thirty pieces of silver for doing nothing. Evil had entered his heart. He smothered the recognition that he was betraying Jesus.

Caiaphas knew what Judas was thinking. He knew that Judas was wrong. He wrung his hands in gleeful anticipation. Jesus was finally in his hands.

ROCCO LEONARD MARTINO

Chapter Eight
Pontius Pilate

The journey from Caesarea had been tedious. The distance was not great, but travelling through the high lands of Judea had always been difficult. Pontius Pilate was weary, since the trip had taken a long time. They were delayed by the fact that Pontius Pilate's wife, Claudia Procula, had insisted on accompanying him so that she could take part in the festivities of Passover in Jerusalem. Her sedia[2] had slowed the entire procession down. Pontius Pilate had decided to ride on horseback rather than in a sedia. He did not want to telegraph any weakness whatsoever. Pontius Pilate was travelling to Jerusalem because he feared difficulty during the celebration of Passover. This feast would attract thousands to Jerusalem, including many Zealots from Galilee. Thank the gods that they had captured Barabbas who was the leader of one of the most violent factions of the Zealots. He would have to deal with him upon his arrival into Jerusalem.

Pontius Pilate had selected two Centurions, Cornelius and Longinus, to accompany him. The Roman Legion was quartered in Caesarea so that the troops that he had with him, commanded by these two Centurions, were considered the best within the entire empire. The garrison in Jerusalem was non-descript, composed mainly of conscripts from the various conquered peoples

---

[2] The sedia was a large chair that had four bulky block like legs, and two supporting arms. It could be screened or curtained.

within the Roman Empire. There were even some Jewish Legionaries. They provided translation capability in dealing with the natives. By and large, however, Greek was sufficient to be understood throughout most of Judea. The common language, of course, was Aramaic, even though Hebrew was common amongst the Jewish people. Pontius Pilate was proficient in Greek, and halting in Aramaic. Since coming to Judea he had made an effort to become proficient in Aramaic, but languages were not a strong point with him.

As he rode, it came to him that the Jews were certainly learned people capable as they were of speaking two or three languages, and reading and writing them as well. They were certainly industrious. That was one of his most difficult problems since they resented the Roman occupation and he was always concerned about plots that would be brewing and that he would have to overcome them one way or another.

Pontius Pilate was under no illusion of the difficulty of his position. Unlike most outer parts of the empire where force was used quite liberally to maintain control, the emperor had decided to allow Herod and his offspring to be kings over segments of Judea, joining with Rome in the exercise of power over the entire country. This had advantages and disadvantages. It was the friendship of Herod with the Emperor Augustine that had initiated this and allowed it to continue under the Emperor Tiberius.

They rode in silence for some time until the ramparts of Jerusalem appeared on the horizon. Pontius Pilate called a halt and had his Centurions come up to him for a short conference.

THE CROSS OF VICTORY

After saluting each other, Pontius Pilate said, "We are almost there. It will be a blessing to proceed to my villa in the heights. That of course will be our unofficial headquarters during our stay in Jerusalem. Officially our headquarters will be at the Praetorian, where you and the Legionaries will be garrisoned. As you know, we are proceeding to Jerusalem at this time mainly because of the celebration of Passover. There has been some unrest amongst the Jews due largely to the efforts at destabilization by the Zealots. They are active mainly in Galilee, but during Passover everybody comes to Jerusalem. Once this celebration is over, and once we have taken care of the Zealot Barabbas who is in the custody of our garrison in Jerusalem, we will return to Caesarea."

He nodded to the Centurions, and paused before continuing.

"Please brace the legionnaires so that we will enter Jerusalem in triumph and not as a group of tired marchers. Have the musicians play a spritely marching song."

With that Pontius Pilate set off on a canter and the two Centurions returned to their positions with the Legionnaires. As the music began, everyone braced and marched spritelier. Suddenly, a tired cohort of Legionnaires became true to their Roman heritage, and began marching with precision and power. It seemed as if an electric current had run through the entire cohort. They were the Roman Legion!

*   *   *

Pontius Pilate had taken a long bath upon arrival at his villa, his unofficial headquarters while he was in Jerusalem. It would certainly be more comfortable than his quarters at the Praetorian. The Legionnaires together with the Centurions had proceeded to the garrison within Jerusalem and were bivouacked there. A small troop of Legionaries had accompanied Pontius Pilate to his residence as guards. These were to be under the command of the Centurion Cornelius. First, Cornelius had to determine the situation in Jerusalem from the resident Tribune and Centurions. With this, he would establish how best to deploy the guard for the security of the Roman Procurator, Pontius Pilate, and his entourage that included his wife. In the interim, the troop would deploy in full guard around the residence.

Centurion Cornelius proceeded to the garrison bivouac where he met with the resident Centurions and proceeded to acquire the intelligence of the situation in Jerusalem.

With this information, he proceeded to the villa of Pontius Pilate to report what he had learned, and to act on it in setting the guard.

"Sir", said Cornelius addressing Pontius Pilate, "Everything is reasonably peaceful in Jerusalem."

After a short pause he added. "There is one difficulty, however. It has to do with a travelling preacher, one Jesus, a carpenter from Nazareth."

"Isn't that in Galilee?" asked Pontius Pilate.

"Yes", said Cornelius. "This man is reported to have cured many people of severe illness, often from birth, and to have raised at least three from the dead."

Pontius Pilate was somewhat surprised. He had not heard of this Jesus. He asked Cornelius, "Why have I not heard of Him before?"

"Probably because He has kept to the hinterland, moving from town to town. While His fame has spread widely amongst the people, it has been a quiet fame. He does not stir up the people. He prays with them. He cures them of their illness. He weeps with them. He asks them to repent of their sins. He says that He forgives them their sins. He has proven to be a man of the people. His only opposition has come from the Pharisees and Sadducees who see Him as a threat to their power. The garrison has told me that the Chief Priest, Caiaphas, is concerned. The rumor is that he is afraid that Jesus will be a threat to his power, and to his income."

"How can this Jesus be a threat to the income of the Chief Priest, Caiaphas?" asked Pontius Pilate.

"Because this Jesus went into the Temple yesterday and toppled the tables of the money-changers and caused a great disturbance, attempting to flog them with His cincture for desecrating the home of His father."

At this phrase Pontius Pilate's eyebrows raised in a quizzical fashion. Then he burst out laughing. "So that pirate Annas has finally been exposed for what he is. The title of Chief Priest is a sham for exerting control over the Jewish people and making a profit at the same time." He shrugged his shoulders. "It's a wonder the Jewish people tolerate such a defilement of their religious beliefs by such a charlatan."

Pilate looked directly at Cornelius, saying nothing further for a few moments, but clearly indicating a certain amount of bafflement. Then he continued.

"I don't completely understand but that doesn't mean that it is not true. I can well understand that the Chief Priest is concerned about any threat to the status quo. I, too, would be concerned but I see no difficulty with public order here. From your remarks I gather that there is no difficulty with Jesus concerning any potential revolt or the stirring up of the people. Is that true Cornelius?"

"Yes, sir!" Cornelius paused and then went on, "There are no reports of any kind that Jesus has done anything other than to reinforce the status of the Emperor as head of state. In fact, there are reports that He was challenged by the Pharisees who presented Him with a coin bearing the head of Caesar Augustus asking Jesus to define who was to be followed. He very adroitly said, 'Render unto Caesar that which is Caesar's and unto God that which is God's'. This has been a common thread in His preaching around the countryside."

"Then I can see that He is not a threat to the public order. Would you agree Cornelius with what you have heard from the garrison?"

"Yes, sir! I agree that Jesus is no threat to the public order. The only threat to Rome is that movement loosely characterized as the Zealots. They are headquartered mainly in Galilee but we have captured one of the most prominent and violent leaders of that group, one called Barabbas. As you know, we are set to try him and execute him at your convenience, sir."

Both remained in deep thought for a moment. Then Pontius Pilate nodded briefly, dismissing the Centurion. Cornelius saluted, took his leave, and left.

Chapter Nine
Caiaphas Plants the Seed

When Caiaphas learned that Pontius Pilate was in residence in Jerusalem, he sent word requesting a meeting with him as soon as possible.

It was the next day before a reply was received inviting Caiaphas to come to the residence in the mid-afternoon. It was Wednesday.

Caiaphas proceeded to the residence of Pontius Pilate alone, but protected by Temple guards as he rode in his sedia.

As he arrived at the residence, he was shown into the atrium where he waited a few minutes. Pontius Pilate came out and greeted him, not effusively, but somewhat stiffly and formally, as befitting the position of Procurator of Judea.

"And so, Caiaphas, I would have thought that you would be too busy with preparations for Passover to seek an audience with me today. It must be something important."

Caiaphas was at his most obsequious best, "Your Excellency. Welcome to Jerusalem. I trust that your visit here will be most propitious and that you will find the Passover celebrations agreeable. While you are not a member of our faith, I think that you will be able to enjoy the festivities for what they are, a joyous celebration."

Pontius Pilate remained silent, nodding as if to agree and accept what Caiaphas had said.

Then Caiaphas took on a more severe look and in his most statesman-like posture added, "I have sought this audience with you because there is a problem with the civil order, a threat of future disturbance."

With the words civil order, Pontius Pilate stiffened and directed a piercing look at Caiaphas.

"What do you mean disturbance to the civil order?" demanded Pontius Pilate.

Without backing down at all, and quite directly, Caiaphas went on to describe the work of Jesus in the surrounding sections of Judea during the past three years and His triumphant entry into Jerusalem on Sunday and His subsequent flogging of the money-changers the next day. He described how Jesus had taken thongs of leather and welded them into a whip and used them to whip the money-changers as He upset their tables and as He scattered their doves and lambs that were held for purchase. Caiaphas was startled when Pontius Pilate burst into laughter.

"Those scoundrels deserved it," said Pontius Pilate, still laughing. "That scoundrel of a father-in-law of yours, even though he was a former Chief Priest, is nothing but a thief. He manipulates everything and everybody for his own profit. His charges to the money-changers and to the peddlers of lambs for sacrifice must be outrageous." Pontius Pilates' laughter subsided and he became somewhat more serious. "I must admit, this Jesus took things into His own hands. Perhaps there is some potential civil disturbance but I don't see any in merely the outrage that He would have at seeing how His fellow Jews are fleeced by Annas."

Caiaphas was taken aback. He had a serious situation here. It was necessary for him to convince Pontius Pilate that Jesus was a threat. At the same time, he had to maintain Pilate's support for his actions and

THE CROSS OF VICTORY

plan, without losing support for his position. He walked a narrow line. He tried another approach. He had to prepare Pilate to execute Jesus without diminishing his own position.

"Excellency, I briefly related the fact that He entered Jerusalem almost in triumph. I should have related the fact that He was also accompanied by hundreds of followers all shouting 'Hosanna' and waving palm fronds. It was the triumphant entry of a King!"

"King!" said Pontius Pilate in surprise.

"Yes, King! That is how He is looked upon by His followers. He claims that His Kingdom is not of this world but that He is the King."

Pontius Pilate became silent. He seemed to ponder the word "King" deeply. Looking directly at Caiaphas he asked "And what do you propose doing?"

"Excellency, I would like to have Him arrested and brought to trial," said Caiaphas. Then he deftly added, "You should consider His execution before He can consolidate His support and challenge Roman authority."

Pilate was not surprised. He knew Caiaphas was a scheming scoundrel who tried to use Roman power for his own purposes. He wondered why Caiaphas was so concerned with Jesus. He had heard rumblings of this holy man who cured the sick but that was all to the good. Anything or anyone who kept the people quiet was to be encouraged. Suddenly he realized that what was good for Rome might be bad for Caiaphas. He immediately understood the stratagem of Caiaphas. Inwardly, he applauded the devious scoundrel but outwardly decided to be stern.

Pontius Pilate assumed a very stern look. "And I suppose you want my help in arresting this man. What else do you want?" asked Pontius Pilate somewhat abruptly.

"Excellency, the trial would be before the Sanhedrin. We would not, of course, involve you unless it is a matter of civil order and potential treachery associated with the rule of Rome." In his most obsequious manner Caiaphas continued, "Excellency, we seek only to preserve the civil order, and to ensure that Roman rule remains in a tranquil and orderly mode." Pontius Pilate laughed again. This time it was somewhat derisive. "Caiaphas, you have something up your sleeve. I think you are afraid of this man, afraid that He is affecting your income and your power base. So be it. But if there is any potential that He is a threat to Rome, then He will certainly be executed. If He is not a threat to Rome, then He will be freed. Go ahead and arrest Him if you wish. Be it upon you. I will not permit Roman soldiers to be part of this arrest."

"Excellency," pleaded Caiaphas, "without the assistance of Roman soldiers there can be no guarantee that the arrest can be executed without disturbance. For that reason we have taken measures to find a time when Jesus will be relatively alone, and certainly away from crowds of His followers. We expect that the arrest will take place after midnight on Thursday."

Pontius Pilate looked quizzically at Caiaphas. "You must have a traitor, someone who will betray Jesus when He is alone. Is that so?"

"Yes. We have someone who will tell us when Jesus is relatively alone and where He is at that time, and has also agreed to lead us to Him, and to identify Him with a kiss on the cheek for those arresters who do not know Him."

Pontius Pilate smiled. Caiaphas was as devious as he believed. He changed his mind. Under these circumstances he saw no problem in allowing Roman soldiers to accompany the Temple guards in this arrest.

With a wave of his hand he dismissed Caiaphas with the words "So be it! I will inform the Tribune to await information from you as to the time of arrest sometime late Thursday evening." And with that Pontius Pilate left the room. Smiling inwardly, knowing that he had achieved his objective, Caiaphas left.

Pilate walked over to a chair in the living area and sat down. He pondered the meeting in his mind. Whenever the Chief Priest came, he was up to something that was not necessarily good for Rome. In this case, Caiaphas wanted his cooperation in arresting and the executing this holy man Jesus. Why? The supposition was that He was a threat to Rome. In reality He must be a threat to Caiaphas. But could He also be a threat to Rome. If so, He certainly had to be executed. What was one Jew more or less to be executed? Pilate smiled inwardly. If he could execute them all, he would have no more problems! He gave a short grunt as he continued musing over the situation. Passover was a time when Jerusalem was six times its size with all the visitors. He could not afford any disturbance.

Just at this point in his musing, his wife, Claudia Procula, came in looking for him.

"What did that terrible man want?" she asked.

Pilate laughed. "Nothing really," he evaded. While he loved his wife, she had no business getting involved in affairs of state. Yet, over the years, her counsel had been excellent. She had a knack of seeing through people to their true purposes. He was interested in her opinions of the Jews and the Jewish leaders; but at the same time he was somewhat exasperated with the conniving of the Chief Priest in always trying to use him and Rome for his own power and profit purposes. He didn't want to talk about the Jews. He tried to brush aside his wife's potential involvement in a further discussion of the visitor.

"What are your plans for our visit to Jerusalem during this festive time?" he asked in attempting to change the subject.

Claudia was not be dissuaded. She laughed and then smilingly walked over to where he was sitting, bent down, and teasingly shook her finger saying gaily, "Pontius you are trying to change the subject. Now tell me what he wanted."

Pilate laughed. He rose, and quietly told her of his discussion with Caiaphas.

Claudia looked him directly in the eye and said, "Pontius be careful of this man. I had a dream about this Jesus. He is a holy man who helps people. He is no threat to Rome. If anything, by keeping the people happy and quiet, He is helping us in our role as rulers." She stopped and then added quietly, "Pontius, you decide for yourself! Do not be swayed by the manipulations of that man."

Then she twirled gaily, and with a laugh, took him by the arm, and said, "Now about this week….."

Chapter Ten
The Supper

It was Thursday. It was the day of the unleavened bread. In Jewish tradition it was also the day upon which the Passover lamb had to be sacrificed. Jesus had remained in Bethany the night before at the home of his good friend Lazarus. The apostles had stayed nearby.

Jesus sent for Peter and John. When they came He said to them, "Go and make preparations for us to eat the Passover."

They were somewhat surprised at this directive and asked, "Where do you want us to prepare for it?"

He replied, "As you enter the city, a man carrying a jar of water will meet you. Follow him to the house that he enters and say to the owner of the house, 'The teacher asks: where is the guest room, where I may eat the Passover with my disciples?' He will show you a large room upstairs, all furnished. Make preparations there."

They were somewhat surprised, but not totally. It was not the first time that they had been given such instructions. Most recently, of course, had been the instruction to proceed into Jerusalem and find the young colt which they then brought to Jesus for His ride into Jerusalem.

They immediately proceeded into Jerusalem and followed Jesus' directive. As He had told them, they found the man carrying the jar and followed him and proceeded to complete the arrangements for the first Passover supper in the upper room of the house. The house was the home of John Mark, a disciple.

* * *

When evening came, the apostles began to assemble in the upper room. Jesus was the last to arrive. In the usual fashion, they greeted each other and spent considerable time exchanging thoughts and opinions, most of which centered around the teachings of Jesus.

In a somewhat jocular fashion, but yet full of meaning, the apostles began to question who would be the most important and in what order in the forthcoming Kingdom promised by Jesus.

Jesus was not amused. In a very serious way, He reprimanded them quietly, but effectively, when He reminded them that throughout His preaching He had always stressed the fact that the one who shall be first shall be last, and the one who shall be last shall be first.

They became quite subdued at this. Judas seemed more subdued than usual. He had a somewhat guilty look about him as if he had done something wrong and was trying to hide it. Jesus looked at him piercingly. Judas had the sense that Jesus knew exactly what he had done. He tried to put on a nonchalant air, but did not succeed. In order to give himself time to compose himself, he drifted to the outer fringes of the group.

Judas had always been a loner amongst the apostles so they were not surprised when he did not take an active part in the spirited discussion. But yet, in a sense, they were. He seemed even more distant than usual.

The room was strangely set up. There were towels and buckets of water and a large basin at one end of the table. Mary, Mary Magdalene, and a few other women disciples had prepared the meal, and they would serve it, but in the manner of the times, would not recline at table. There was bread and wine and bitter herbs, but no lamb. There were thirteen places around the table. A slightly elevated one for the host was not in the center of the thirteen, but the second from the end. The apostles were puzzled. They discussed amongst themselves that this did not seem to be a Seder, but rather a formal dinner of some kind. When Jesus had not arrived promptly after they did, they continued discussing their experiences travelling with Jesus during the past few months. The miracles were a common topic, and a continual wonderment at the power He exercised. This was especially so in the raising of the dead, most particularly, the calling of Lazarus from the tomb four days after he had been buried.

There was no doubt in their minds that He was certainly a king. He had to be the son of God to exercise such power. They began initially before His arrival in a jocular fashion as to who would have the most importance in the Kingdom of God. Then it became somewhat more serious as they contended who was the most important and who had done the most. It was at that point that Jesus came into their midst. He quietly rebuked them for showing ambition and then removed His outer garment, and moving to the towels and the large basin filled it with water and asked each of them to come in turn so He could wash their feet. There was great hesitancy in this, but they did come, except for Peter, who held back. When Jesus had washed the feet of the other eleven, He called to Peter who declined to come saying, "You will never wash my feet, Lord."

Jesus smiled and very quietly and directly said to Peter, "Unless I wash your feet, you will never have eternal life."

Peter immediately came over and said, "Lord, wash not only my feet but my hands and face." Peter was subdued after that, realizing that he had totally misunderstood the lesson that Jesus had taught them. By His actions in washing their feet immediately after their contention as to who would become the greater or more important in the Kingdom of God, Peter realized, as all of them realized, the actual acting out of the continual message of Jesus, "He who shall be first shall be last, and he shall be last who shall be first." Self-pride and self-importance were something that Jesus would not tolerate. He sought the most humble and, finding him, elevated him to importance.

Seeking to reinforce his love for Jesus, Peter gratuitously said to him, "Lord I will never deny you."

Jesus smiled. While it pained Him because He well recognized the earnestness of Peter, He thought it best to tell him, "Peter, before the cock crows you will deny me three times."

Peter was stunned; there was no way that could happen. It was merely Jesus needling him because of his resistance to having his feet washed. Peter could not understand it, but then again he was beginning to get an inkling. Jesus wanted him to clearly understand that he was to be a servant of the others and not their master. As a servant, he could lead the church.

Just at that point Jesus stunned them all. They all had had great fear and apprehension of coming to Jerusalem that somehow or other the Chief Priest would have Jesus arrested and executed. So far this fear had been groundless but had still not left them. Jesus, in a very direct way, said, "One of you has betrayed me. As I have told you repeatedly, I expect to be arrested and executed while I am here in Jerusalem. This has been made possible by betrayal of one of you.

They all began to murmur amongst themselves as to who it was.

After some time in such discussion, the time had come for the meal. Jesus and the apostles took their places at the table. Judas took the place of honor at the right of Jesus and John sat on His left. The other apostles took places around the table with Peter taking the very last place, in the most humble fashion.

As the hubbub of seating settled down, and everyone sat quietly around the table, Jesus once more reminded them that He had predicted His imminent death. He went so far as to say, "I have eagerly desired to eat this Passover meal with you before I suffer. Because I tell all of you I will never eat it again until it finds its fulfillment in the Kingdom of God."

The apostles were shaken. While they had heard Jesus on many occasions predict His arrest and execution, they had never taken it seriously. They knew that He was a target of many different forces, most especially those of the Chief Priest. He would be a threat to the status quo since He was continually challenging the lack of compassion and forgiveness on their part. He had, on more than one occasion, attacked the Sadducees, who were the controlling force in the Sanhedrin, the governing body of the Jews. The episode three days ago when He had upset the tables of the money-changers in the Temple would certainly not have endeared Him to the Temple authorities, they suspected that the Chief

Priest was fomenting some kind of plot against Jesus. What surprised them, and made them apprehensive, was the sudden realization that this was somewhat imminent, not a far-off event.

Jesus smiled as He saw the arrangements and said nothing. The conversation continued and they pressed Him as to who would betray them. Jesus said that he who shared the dipping of the bread was the man who would do so. Doing this He took a piece of bread and dipped it in the dish, at which point Judas did also. Judas, in a very insincere fashion said, "Is it I, Lord?" Jesus looked at him and said, "It is as you say."

The others had been busy in their discussion and had not noticed this exchange. But Judas noticed it completely. He now understood that Jesus knew. Jesus said to him, "Be quick about what you are going to do. Do it!"

Judas said to Jesus, "Master, what are your plans after this dinner?"

"As you know, Judas, one of my favorite places to pray is Gethsemane. I will proceed there to pray after. If you leave and wish to find me afterwards, I will be there."

With that, Jesus looked knowingly at Judas and said, "You had better go now to do what you have to do and want to do. Do it now!"

Judas rose from the table and left to tell the Chief Priest where and when Jesus would be relatively isolated from His disciples.

The apostles were somewhat surprised at this sudden departure by Judas. After a short discussion they came to the conclusion that he had left to distribute alms to the poor. Jesus had remained silent during this discussion.

Jesus turned to John and engaged him in a detailed conversation concerning the various miracles and signs that He had performed and the teachings and discussions that He had with the Pharisees and the Sadducees. He asked John about the impact of His teachings and acts upon the people. This began a discussion once again amongst all of the apostles. This time there was no talk of who would have the most senior position in the Kingdom to come.

Then Jesus rose to speak to them. There was instant silence. He reminded them that He had often foretold His own betrayal and execution in Jerusalem. For that reason He had delayed His entry into Jerusalem until His time had come. His time had come now. This was the last time that they would dine together.

There were cries of "No, no!" around the table. While somewhat apprehensive for some time previous about this entry into Jerusalem, His apostles were not prepared to realize that this was their last supper together. Jesus raised His hand and there was instant silence. Then He reached to the table and picked up a loaf of bread and broke it into pieces. He gave each of the apostles a piece of bread and each time He said, "This is my body, which is given for you. Do this in remembrance of me."

Then He reached for the chalice and took it to each of them and before asking them to drink from the chalice, He said, "This is my blood of the new testament, which is shed for many. Verily I say unto you, I will drink no more of the fruit of the vine, until that day that I drink it new in the Kingdom of God."

Now the apostles understood. Jesus was leaving them. But He was leaving them His body and His blood which was to be consumed in a meeting of the followers in the future. Whenever they broke bread and drank wine they would be eating His body and drinking His blood. That was the gift of Jesus. Jesus was silent for a moment or two. He had their instant attention.

Jesus then began to tell them how important it was to travel through life independent of the need for wealth. As He put it, it would be possible to travel without "neither script nor shoes." They understood.

"Carry no purse, no bag, no sandals; and salute no one on the road. Whatever house you enter, first say, 'Peace be to this house!' And if a son of peace is there, your peace shall rest upon him; but if not, it shall return to you. And remain in the same house, eating and drinking what they provide, for the laborer deserves his wages; do not go from house to house. Whenever you enter a town and they receive you, eat what is set before you; heal the sick in it and say to them, 'The Kingdom of God has come near to you.' But whenever you enter a town and they do not receive you, go into its streets and say, 'Even the dust of your town that clings to our feet, we wipe off against you; nevertheless know this, that the Kingdom of God has come near.' I tell you, it shall be more tolerable on that day for Sodom than for that town."

"A new commandment I give to you, that you love one another; even as I have loved you, that you also love one another. By this all men will know that you are my disciples, if you have love for one another."

The apostles were overwhelmed with feelings of love on one kind and anguish on the other. They loved Jesus. He had shown His love for them in many different ways. In the same fashion, He had shown His love for so many people, taking upon Himself their sufferings and anguish. He had fed the hungry, cured the sick, and even raised the dead to life. He had now foretold His own betrayal and death. He had told them that He would never dine with them again. They knew He believed it. They hoped it would not happen.

They were all now pretty certain that Judas was the one who would betray Jesus. His mere rapid departure earlier in the meal surely indicated that he was about some nefarious deed. They hoped he would fail, but, based upon the statements of Jesus, they were fearful and apprehensive that he would succeed.

As a group they virtually said, "Master, let us hope this cup can pass from you. Let us hope that we will dine again in this life just as we know we will dine again in the life to come."

Jesus smiled. Then He told them that He wanted them to go with Him to the Garden of Gethsemane to pray. With Him they walked across the Kidron Valley.

Jesus and the eleven left the room, and as they did so Peter looked back in deep thought. The Lord had asked Him to head His church after He was gone. Peter was beginning to understand the magnitude of this undertaking, and how indeed it was his responsibility to serve the others. He understood the ceremony of the breaking of the bread and the drinking of the wine. He knew that from this point forward the followers of Jesus would be identified by the breaking of bread.

ROCCO LEONARD MARTINO

Chapter Eleven
The Arrest

Jesus and His apostles walked across the valley to the garden of Gethsemane. They had often prayed there in the past, but there was something different about tonight. It was not only the late hour, but also the mood of Jesus which He telegraphed to His followers.

When they arrived, Jesus asked them to wait for Him at the gate while He proceeded to pray alone. Walking a short distance from them, He threw himself on the ground and prayed earnestly, devoutly, and hard to His father in heaven. He said, "Abba, Father, for you all things are possible; remove this cup from me; yet, not what I want, but what you want."

He prayed so hard that sweat and blood came to His brow. He knew what was to come. He did not shirk it, but the human nature did have to ask if the cup could pass.

After a somewhat prolonged period of prayer, He rose and went to His followers. He came and found them sleeping; and He said to Peter, "Simon, are you asleep? Could you not keep awake one hour? Keep awake and pray that you may not come into the time of trial; the spirit indeed is willing, but the flesh is weak." And again He went away and prayed, saying the same words. And once more He came and found them sleeping, for their eyes were very heavy; and they did not know what to say to Him. He came a third time and said to them, "Are you still sleeping and taking your rest? Enough! The hour has come; the Son of Man is betrayed into the hands of sinners. Get up, let us be going. See, my betrayer is at hand."

Suddenly there was noise in the air. There was a clamor as of a large group of people approaching the garden, and the sight of many lanterns. As the apostles looked, they saw that there was a crowd of Roman soldiers, Temple guards, servants of the high Priests, and a number of the followers of Caiaphas, most especially the money-changers and the merchants from the Temple. They were led by Judas.

As the crowd descended upon the garden, they walked right past the drowsy, but waking, followers of Jesus and, led by Judas, went directly to Jesus. Jesus rose and confronted the group. Judas walked toward Him and kissed Him on the cheek. Then Jesus, knowing all that was to happen to Him, came forward and asked them, "Whom are you looking for?" They answered, "Jesus of Nazareth." Jesus replied, "I am He." Judas, who betrayed him, was standing with them. When Jesus said to them, "I am He," they stepped back and fell to the ground. Again He asked them, "Whom are you looking for?" And they said, "Jesus of Nazareth." Jesus answered, "I told you that I am He. So if you are looking for me, let these men go." This was to fulfill the word that He had spoken, "I did not lose a single one of those whom you gave me."

With that Jesus turned away from Judas and faced the Roman soldiers. They immediately chained His legs and feet so that He could barely move. They handled Him roughly. One of them even spat upon Him. He was being treated as a common criminal. At this point, Peter, who was fully aroused and angry at the treatment being accorded Jesus, took out his sword and attacked;

severing the ear of one of the servants of the Chief Priest.

Jesus rebuked him. Then Jesus said to them, "Have you come out with swords and clubs to arrest me as though I were a bandit? Day after day I was with you in the Temple teaching, and you did not arrest me. But let the scriptures be fulfilled." Then, taking the ear of the servant of the high Priest, He put it back on his head and it was immediately healed.

Now that Jesus was totally incapacitated, chained, and totally in their power, the guards marched Him back to the residence of the high Priest. In this case it was to that of Annas. This had been pre-arranged with Caiaphas to try and confuse Jesus into admissions.

When they arrived at the residence of Annas, the Roman guards took their leave, since the agreement between the high Priest and Pontius Pilate had been that the Roman guards would assist in the arrest, but once arrested, Jesus was to be left in the custody of the Temple guards.

Then Annas questioned Jesus about His disciples and about His teaching. Jesus answered, "I have spoken openly to the world; I have always taught in synagogues and in the Temple, where all the Jews come together. I have said nothing in secret. Why do you ask me? Ask those who heard what I said to them; they know what I said." When He had said this, one of the guards standing nearby struck Jesus on the face, saying, "Is that how you answer, Annas?" Jesus answered, "If I have spoken wrongly, testify to the wrong. But if I have spoken rightly, why do you strike me?"

Annas decided it would be best to have Jesus tried by Caiaphas. Annas sent Him bound to the Chief Priest.

When Jesus was brought before Caiaphas, the Chief Priest was determined to have Jesus tricked or coerced into admissions that would allow Him to be found guilty. The hour was well after midnight, so Caiaphas deferred the final trial of Jesus until the morning when he would summon the Sanhedrin.

This encounter with Caiaphas was observed by Peter in the courtyard. It was chilly and some fires had been lit. Peter, who had followed the soldiers with the arrested Jesus, went to warm himself by the fire. He was immediately identified as one of the Galileans that had been a follower of Jesus. He vehemently denied this. Then another serving girl also accused him. He denied this as well. He turned and went to walk away when another came up to him, and accused him of being a Galilean follower of Jesus. He was in the process of vehemently denying this, his third denial of Jesus, when suddenly a cock crowed. It was at that point that Jesus was led by the soldiers, treating Him very roughly, taking Him to an imprisonment place to await His trial in the early morning before the Sanhedrin. Jesus looked at Peter knowingly as He walked by. Peter immediately burst into tears and suddenly realized that he had denied Jesus three times, as foretold. He would remember this in the years to come up until his death, recognizing the frailty of humanity and the constant need for repentance and forgiveness. He knew that Jesus forgave him, but it did not diminish his own deep regret at having denied Jesus – not once, but three times!

Chapter Twelve
Trial Before the Sanhedrin

The Sanhedrin met at an early hour. Nicodemus and Joseph of Arimathea were present. Both disputed strongly with Caiaphas when they learned that there had been a preliminary trial the night before. They reminded Caiaphas that trials that were binding could not be held at night, and that any trial that might lead to execution had to have an interval of at least one day between the different sessions. In other words, by the very mitzvot, or the code of law of the Jewish religion, any trial leading to an execution had to span at least two days. Hence, as the dissidents of Caiaphas pointed out, this trial had no legal basis before Judaic law.

Caiaphas brushed aside their objections. He promised to have them escorted from the meeting. They proceeded to gain support from others, at which point Caiaphas called the guards and had all of them removed.

Now that Caiaphas had the Sanhedrin reduced to only his supporters, he proceeded to interrogate Jesus. Now the Chief Priests and the whole council were looking for false testimony against Jesus so that they might put Him to death, but they found none, though many false witnesses came forward. At last two came forward and said, "This fellow said, 'I am able to destroy the Temple of God and to build it in three days.'" The Chief Priest stood up and said, "Have you no answer? What is it that they testify against you?" But Jesus was silent. Then the Chief Priest said to Him, "I put you under oath before the living God, tell us if you are the

Messiah, the Son of God." Jesus said to Him, "You have said so. But I tell you, from now on you will see the Son of Man seated at the right hand of Power and coming on the clouds of heaven."

Then the Chief Priest tore His clothes and said, "He has blasphemed! Why do we still need witnesses? You have now heard His blasphemy. What is your verdict?" They answered, "He deserves death." Then they spat in His face and struck Him; and some slapped Him, saying, "Prophesy to us, you Messiah! Who is it that struck you?"

Annas and Caiaphas then conducted an intensive conversation between themselves, out of the hearing of the other members of the Sanhedrin. "We've got Him!" said Caiaphas. "Don't be too sure," said Annas. "We don't dare execute Him because we don't have enough supporters to insulate ourselves from the followers of Jesus who are very numerous here in Jerusalem at this time. In addition, we don't have much of a case. There are many who would say that Jesus is the son of God because of the miracles that He has performed. Nobody can raise people from the dead, if they are not divine!"

"Rubbish!" said Caiaphas. "He is a trickster."

"If He's a trickster, then how can He hold his own, showing great learning, in the Synagogue and in the Temple? In dispute after dispute He has shown that He truly does understand the scriptures."

"I didn't say He didn't know His scriptures, I'm saying He is a trickster," insisted Caiaphas. Caiaphas became silent and then, suddenly, looked up at Annas and said, "If indeed He is the son of God, then He can escape our power at any time. If, on the other hand, He cannot escape our power and His execution, then He is a trickster."

Annas shook his head. "I am older than you. I am equally concerned about the effect Jesus has upon our authority and upon our income," Annas said, referring to the money-changers tables and the subsequent disarray of important sales during the Passover preparation. "But, something tells me there is more to Jesus than your claim of Him being a trickster. His deeds are too many, and too extensive to be those merely of someone who, somehow or other, can manipulate things to give an illusion of a miracle. I think they were real miracles, Caiaphas. So we had best be careful." Annas remained silent and then his greed and fear took hold. He had worked too long and too hard to maintain his power and that of his five sons. Now his son-in-law, whom he continually tried to manipulate in the office of Chief Priest, was proving more resistant to his directives than his five sons had been. The ultimate fear, of course, was Rome. If things got a little unstable Rome would intercede and wipe them all away. Some twenty years ago he had been Chief Priest, but had angered Rome and he had been removed almost overnight. Thankfully, his manipulations had made it possible to maintain the role of high Priest within his family. How best to overcome the fear of Rome? It was obvious. Have the Romans execute Jesus. Now if only Caiaphas would come to the same conclusion. Apparently he had.

"Annas, sire," said Caiaphas. "I have an idea. If we get Rome to execute Jesus, then they can take the brunt of the ill favor of the Jewish people because it is Rome that will have executed their hero and not us. We can stand firm with our people and the fact that we found Him guilty, and we can stand firm with others that it was the Romans who executed Jesus and not us."

"Good idea," agreed Annas, looking at Caiaphas with knowledgeable understanding of the devious nature of his son-in-law, "And I'm sure that you've already planted that seed in the mind Pontius Pilate." Caiaphas laughed. Looking towards the Sanhedrin in the other room, he said to Annas, "We'd better get back or they will be wondering what we are conspiring over. Let's take Jesus to Pontius Pilate and let me do the talking." With that, they went back into the meeting room with the Sanhedrin and suggested that they would now proceed to take Jesus for final trial and disposition to the home of Pontius Pilate. They used as their reason the fact of the Passover coming the following day, which would be the Sabbath. As such, it would be impossible to have a two-day trial, since it would carry over into the Sabbath and the celebration of Passover. The execution of Jesus would then be deferred for some time. However, if they proceeded to have the Romans try Jesus and, if they found Him guilty, execute Him, it could be done this day, and it could be done before the Sabbath began at sundown.

There was some question raised by members of the Sanhedrin that as they proceeded to the praetorian and entered, then they would be defiled and it would not be possible for them to celebrate the Passover. Caiaphas knowingly smiled and said that he would ensure that any hearing before Pontius Pilate would be held in his courtyard and not in the praetorian proper so that they would not be defiled.

Caiaphas called the Chief guard and told him to send an emissary to Pontius Pilate to request an immediate trial for a criminal that potentially had to be executed this day, before Passover. Caiaphas was bringing the Sanhedrin with him in case Pontius Pilate would want to call any witnesses and he would ask the forbearance and the granting of a special favor by Pontius Pilate of conducting the trial in the courtyard so that he and his other traditional Jews would not be defiled by entering the praetorian and would be able to eat the Passover dinner. Otherwise they would not. As he explained this to the guard, he could not help smiling inwardly at how he was manipulating Pontius Pilate, even to the point of having him conduct a trial in his courtyard rather than in his regular meeting room. That is the ultimate of manipulation. Have someone give up their own premises where they have full control and come to you. In this case coming to the courtyard of the praetorian was, in a sense, coming to Caiaphas. Caiaphas laughed. He told the guard to use the usual niceties such as entreaty, and everything else to impress upon the governor the importance of having this trial immediately. He told the guard to provide the governor with his deep regrets at such short notice of this request, but he hoped that it would be approved. He told the guard to wait for a reply from Pontius Pilate before having the other guards bring Jesus to the courtyard.

As they began to make preparations to move Jesus for trial by Pontius Pilate, Caiaphas called aside the captain of the Temple guard and instructed him as follows: "Make sure that we are surrounded by our own people. Make sure further that the courtyard of Pontius Pilate has none of Jesus' followers. Our most logical approach would be to have the money-changers and the merchants from the Temple grounds fill the courtyard so that others cannot be there. It is important that this entire group of people be our people under our control who will do exactly as we wish. In fact, if any of the followers of Jesus try to insert themselves, make sure that they are silenced no matter what happens. Do you understand?"

The guard nodded. "Yes, Sir," saluted and left. Caiaphas then proceeded to lead his selected group of people to the square in front of the praetorian.

Chapter Thirteen
Caiaphas Plotting the Execution of Jesus

Caiaphas was elated, yet concerned. He had Jesus in his custody, and he had grounds to have Him executed under Judaic law, but even that was somewhat uncertain. Under Judaic law, the trial had been improper. No execution could be carried out until at least another meeting of the Sanhedrin, the full Sanhedrin, at least twenty-four hours after the meeting that had just ended. The reaction of the full Sanhedrin was uncertain. There would definitely be a significant group that would oppose execution. If word of what they were doing escaped to the people, there might even be an uprising. The very uprising that he was accusing Jesus of possibly fomenting, would actually occur, fomented not by Jesus but by Caiaphas himself. If the Romans suddenly realized his role in this, they would be ruthless in deposing him as Chief Priest, and the possibility of execution could not be ruled out. Caiaphas was on dangerous ground.

He felt pressed on all sides. The popularity of Jesus and the attack by Jesus upon the money-changers and merchants associated with the Temple were a direct threat to his authority and to his income. He could not allow that to continue. On the other hand, as the popularity of Jesus increased, this would certainly lead to disturbances that would lead the Romans to intervene and quite probably blame the Chief Priest for being unable to control his people. That, in turn, was a threat to his position, if not his life.

As Caiaphas had told the Sanhedrin repeatedly, it would be better for one man to be executed then for the whole nation to suffer. Jesus had to go!

In the midst of his musing while waiting for word from Pontius Pilate to proceed to bring Jesus to him, the guard entered and said that Judas wished to see him. Caiaphas was startled. He never expected to see Judas ever again. With thirty pieces of silver he was a somewhat wealthy man. He told the guard to bring Judas in.

It was a distraught Judas who entered. He no longer swaggered. He threw himself down on his knees before Caiaphas, clasping his hands; he looked up at Caiaphas with tear-stained eyes and said, "You must forgive me. I have sinned terribly, and done a terrible injustice. Jesus is a holy man. He is from God. I've betrayed Him to you. I'm returning the thirty pieces of silver in the hope that you will now not only forgive me, but forgive Jesus. With the return of this money, our pact is dissolved. You have no right to have Jesus. I implore you to release Him."

Caiaphas laughed in derision. "You foolish man, there is no way that Jesus will be released by me."

Caiaphas pondered quickly. There is no way he should or could indicate to Judas in any way his own concerns about a Jesus who was free. He had to maintain his posture and position that Jesus has blasphemed and as such was to be executed. "Jesus has blasphemed. He is to be executed. We are on our way now to confirm this sentence of death by the governor. Your request is denied. Take your money and go. You have been paid more than you are worth. Go!"

THE CROSS OF VICTORY

Judas rose. The enormity of his betrayal increased in magnitude in his mind. He took the money bag from his belt and threw it at the feet of Caiaphas and screamed at the top of his voice, "Here is your money! It is you that prize money above all else. I've seen my sin. I've seen what wrong I have done. You have not."

And with that Judas ran from the room.

Judas ran from the Temple. He did not stop running until he came to the Valley of Hinnom. Finding a suitable tree, he removed the sash around his garments, tied one end around his neck, and standing on a huge boulder, brought the other end around the tree. Then he stepped off the boulder.

The wind coming down the valley moved the body back and forth until Judas strangled and died.

Caiaphas looked hard at the departing Judas, with qualms suddenly emerging in his heart. Judas had been right and struck hard at a hidden element of his soul. He was a Priest. But this moment of remorse passed quickly. Yes, he was a Priest but he had to uphold the Judaic law. Cloaking himself in the mechanism of the law, he stilled the doubts in his heart. He also stilled any apprehension he had as to the final outcome.

While this tragic end to the life of Judas was unfolding, Caiaphas had returned to where Judas had thrown the money pouch onto the floor of the Temple. He retrieved it and tossed it up and down in his hand as he tried to decide what to do with it. Calling one of his attendants, he told him to take the money and to buy the potter's field where indigent persons would be buried. From that day forward this became known as the Field of Blood. He paced for a few more minutes deep in thought.

Just at that moment the guard entered and told him that word had been received and that Jesus was to be brought before Pontius Pilate. The governor had also indicated that he would conduct the interview in the courtyard so that the members of the Sanhedrin, who accompanied Caiaphas, and Caiaphas himself, would not be defiled so that they would be capable of eating the Paschal Lamb.

Caiaphas smiled. His planning had succeeded. And now to bring off the rest of the victory.

Chapter Fourteen
The First Trial before Pontius Pilate

Jesus was brought from the cell into which He had been thrown to spend what was left of the night after His trial before the Sanhedrin. The guards had abused and mocked Him; some had even spat upon Him.

As He was brought out into the light, He seemed tired, but His spirit did not appear broken. As the guards led Him past Caiaphas, Caiaphas glared at Him. Jesus returned his glare with a look of sympathy, almost as if He was saying, "I forgive you!"

Caiaphas was surprised. In any event, he followed the caravan of guards escorting Jesus under their control. They were accompanied by the horde of supporters whom Caiaphas and Annas had recruited to surround Jesus. In that fashion they could exclude normal citizens from the proceedings in Pontius Pilate's courtyard.

As they proceeded they kept noise to a minimum so as not to alert any citizens who may have wondered at what was going on. They were careful to surround Jesus so that the prisoner could not be seen or identified by anyone outside their circle. Every measure of this sort was necessary in order to preserve the façade that Caiaphas would be presenting to Pontius Pilate.

When they were totally assembled in the courtyard of the governor, the guards informed him, and he made his appearance. He strode in purposely in his full regalia as a Roman governor. He was surrounded by a number of Legionaries, also in full regalia. He was also attended by a Centurion. He strode forward to Caiaphas and in a strong voice asked, "Now what do you want? Who are you bringing for me to judge, and why are you doing this without prior notice?"

Caiaphas proceeded to tell Pontius Pilate of the realities of the pending Passover celebration and of the Judaic law that made it necessary for capital punishment to be executed only after a suitable trial. In this case, it was impossible for them to conduct the trial since, in their opinion; the crime was one against Rome.

Pontius Pilate seemed puzzled. Looking directly at Caiaphas, he asked, "Is this the man you came to see me about? This man called Jesus, the carpenter from Nazareth?"

"Yes," answered Caiaphas. "This man is causing disturbances all over the countryside and is a threat to our peaceful existence under the benevolent rule of Rome." Pontius Pilate laughed. Continuing with a broad chuckle, he said, "Caiaphas, you are a wily one. If I didn't know you better I would think that you are trying to be humorous."

Then, becoming more serious, he added, "What is this man accused of?"

Caiaphas began, "Since leaving Galilee months ago, He has attracted a group of followers and is proceeding around the countryside."

Pontius Pilate immediately picked up on the word Galilee. "You mean He is a Galilean?"

Somewhat puzzled, Caiaphas answered, "Yes."

Pontius Pilate suddenly saw a way out of the dilemma. He could extricate himself in this battle between Jesus and His followers on one hand, and the

THE CROSS OF VICTORY

Chief Priest on the other. Pontius Pilate was no fool. He had put it together. The prior visits by Caiaphas to his residence with the concocted story of the threat of Jesus to Rome now made sense. Now this Jesus was being brought before him. Rather than be caught in the middle, he could now defer the entire matter to Herod, who was the Tetrarch of Galilee. With a suppressed air of mirth, Pilate, looking directly at Caiaphas, said, "Ah, your man, Jesus, is a Galilean and as such must be judged by Herod." With that, Pilate turned to the Centurion and said, "Cornelius, please provide an escort to take this prisoner to Herod for judgment by him."

Turning to Caiaphas, he said, "Chief Priest, please take your prisoner to Herod, since it is in his jurisdiction that these events occurred so that the trial you are requesting should be conducted by him."

With that Pontius Pilate turned and reentered his residence.

Somewhat taken aback by the entire proceedings, Caiaphas was just standing there until the Centurion suddenly began giving orders to the Legionaries who were present, and almost immediately, another sixteen Legionaries joined the group, surrounded them, and escorted them to the palace of Herod, who happened to be in Jerusalem at this time because he, too, had come to celebrate the Passover there.

ROCCO LEONARD MARTINO

Chapter Fifteen
Herod Antipas, Tetrarch of Galilee

The decision by Pontius Pilate to defer the trial of Jesus to Herod Antipas was one of administrative buck passing. In his opinion, Jesus was innocent. He did not want to succumb to the pressure of Caiaphas and Annas in finding Jesus guilty in order to suit their purposes. He realized that Jesus was a threat to the status quo power base of Caiaphas, but this was of no import to Pontius Pilate. The position of Rome was that the Chief Priest was subservient to Roman authority and was only a useful expedient in the control of the native population by Rome. In this case, since the mitzvoth, that regulated the Jews, combined religious and governing authority in one body, the Sanhedrin, Rome was quite satisfied with the arrangement of appointing the Chief Priest and then ensuring that that person, and that office, were subservient at all times to the policies and needs for governance by Rome.

Pontius Pilate did not really respect Caiaphas. Nor did he fear him. His only fear was Emperor Tiberius. Pontius Pilate did not feel that he was extremely popular or on the good side of Tiberius because of some administrative errors, or some would even say blunders, on his part.

It had all started when he marched into Jerusalem on his initial entry into the city with the standard bearers bearing the image of Caesar. This had thoroughly offended the Jews, who had complained to Tiberius. Before the word could come back from Rome to remove them, Pontius Pilate had become aware of this disturbance and removed the offending images.

But perhaps the most grievous difference came when Pontius Pilate insisted the Temple funds be used in the construction of the aqueduct, bringing more freshwater to Jerusalem. The Temple authorities, most especially in the person of the high Priest, had reacted strongly against this and once again had complained to Tiberius.

Pontius Pilate was quite certain that in the particular case of Jesus, this was a very difficult situation for him. If he ruled against the Sanhedrin, or if he ruled contrary to the plan and desire of Caiaphas, then there would certainly be complaints to Rome and to Tiberius. This could very well be the straw that broke the camel's back between him and Tiberius. He was very concerned that if the ruling went against the wishes of the Sanhedrin, and if, subsequently, there was any kind of riot or disturbance in Jerusalem, or in Judea, attributed to Jesus, then Tiberius would probably come down very hard on Pontius Pilate. In the deepest recesses of his concerns, he was certain that he would be recalled to Rome if, somehow or other, he made the wrong decision here.

If Jesus was executed, all problems were eliminated. Whether guilty or innocent, releasing Jesus created problems; but executing Him solved problems.

This is not a case of the death of one man more or less. There was no doubt in his mind that Jesus was innocent. He was certainly not guilty of anything that would justify His execution. That did not mean that He would not be executed. Pontius Pilate would do what he could to satisfy his conscience, and the note that he had received from his wife so long as it did not place him in an impossible position with regard to Rome. Hence, he thought that his transfer of the case to Herod was a stroke of genius. He awaited the results.

*   *   *

Herod was in a quandary, unknown to Pontius Pilate. His execution of John the Baptist, by decapitation, upon the whim of Salome, his wife's daughter, did not sit too well with his Jewish subjects. They were not pleased, in many different ways, with the manner in which they felt that he was a puppet of Rome, which indeed he was. But still, he tried to maintain the pretext that he was representing the interests of the Jewish people whom he ruled, and that he ruled them in the fashion that would be beneficial to the Jews and not necessarily beneficial to Rome, even though he would satisfy Rome. His entire demeanor was to convince his subjects that he was not a puppet of Rome, but rather a very tough barrier between Rome and themselves.

His execution of John the Baptist had not sat well with his followers because they deemed it to be an act of lust and incest. After a sensuous dance by Salome, his wife's daughter, he had acceded to her request to have the head of John the Baptist brought to her.

And now Pontius Pilate had sent him Jesus.

Herod was pleased when Jesus was brought into his presence. Jesus was escorted by Roman Legionaries, commanded by the Centurion Longinus. Also with them was the scribe Quinus.

Herod had heard much about the work of Jesus throughout Galilee. For a long time he had been desirous of seeing Him, but had never had the opportunity. And yet here He was before him, bound and helpless. Not only that, but he was startled by the stately appearance of Jesus even though He was apparently exhausted. Despite this, Jesus appeared calm and cast a steady, unblinking gaze upon Herod.

For a somewhat prolonged period of time, at least a quarter of an hour, Herod asked Jesus a repeated set of questions which He refused to answer. No matter what Herod asked, Jesus remained silent.

Herod proceeded to taunt Jesus in terms of His ability to perform miracles. He accused Him of trickery and showmanship. He proceeded to downplay all of the miracles as mere staging, an attempt to fool everyone into thinking that He was a prophet. To all of this Jesus remained silent, at all times looking directly at Herod, His eyes boring directly into his soul. Herod could not maintain His glance, and looked away while he continued his diatribe.

After a long period of time with statements in this fashion, Herod decided it would have no avail. He then turned to the Chief Priest who had accompanied Jesus and asked why He was there.

Caiaphas began a long discourse with all of the alleged crimes committed by Jesus. He ended with his description of the act of blasphemy.

Herod listened attentively, the only reaction being the lifting of his eyebrows in astonishment at the revelation of the admission by Jesus that He was the son of God. The thought flashed through his mind quite rapidly that this statement might very well be true. While he had done his utmost to taunt Jesus into the performance of some miracle, he had believed that the miracles of Jesus had really happened. He had cured the sick, He had made the blind to see, He had made the lame to walk, and He had raised people from the dead. This was no ordinary mortal before him. This might very well be the son of God. There was certainly a nobility about this prisoner. He did not act like others. He very well knew what the Chief Priest was attempting to accomplish – His execution by crucifixion. And yet He stood tall, erect, calm, certainly noble, and somewhat awe-inspiring. This was no ordinary mortal.

He called the scribe over to him and said, "Please take a message to your master, Pontius Pilate. Indicate that I have found nothing in my examination of this man that would justify His execution.

With that he turned to Caiaphas and said, "I can understand what you are trying to do, but I do believe that this is outside my jurisdiction, and outside that of Rome. This man has not violated any law of Rome or of my tetrarchy. He may have violated your rules as you govern through the Sanhedrin, but that is your affair. My understanding is that you have the power of execution. If you wish this man executed, then I leave it to you to carry out that penalty. From my point of view, this man is innocent."

With that, Herod gave instructions to return the prisoner to Pontius Pilate, once again summoning the scribe Quinus to deliver his message.

A disappointed, but still undefeated, Caiaphas, followed Jesus and the soldiers as they returned to Pontius Pilate for a final resolution of the fate of Jesus.

ROCCO LEONARD MARTINO

Chapter Sixteen
The Final Trial before Pilate

Jesus was brought back from His trial with Herod to the plaza of the Praetorian. Once again it was Pontius Pilate who came out, so that the Jews would not be defiled by entering the Praetorian.

As Jesus was lead, heavily chained, He was occasionally abused by the soldiers, who took delight in striking Him. At all times, He walked erect and gave no indication that He was subdued in any way. After a number of blows from one soldier in particular, Jesus turned to him and said, "Why do you strike me? I have done nothing to you. You know what I have said throughout Judea. In Jerusalem, in the Temple, and in the marketplace I have said the same thing repeatedly. So why do you strike me? If I have spoken wrongly, testify to the wrong. But if I have spoken rightly, why do you strike me?"

The guard went to strike Jesus again but his hand stopped in mid-air as his eyes met those of Jesus, full of compassion and devoid of all fear. The guard lowered his arm and walked away. The other guards, taking notice of this encounter, also stopped their abuse of Jesus.

The procession moved quickly back to the Praetorian.

Caiaphas was upset that Jesus was leaving Herod so soon. He had been convinced that Herod would find some guilt, and might even have had Jesus executed. He was now concerned that nothing must stand in the way of the execution of Jesus by the Romans. He had to convince Pontius Pilate, one way or another, to find Him guilty of a capital crime.

Caiaphas walked rapidly once he had been informed that Jesus would be tried almost immediately. He ran over in his mind all of the steps that had to be taken. First and foremost, he had to ensure that the crowd in the immediate vicinity of the Praetorian's courtyard would be in favor of the execution of Jesus. He gave immediate orders to his attendants who accompanied him to inform the money-changers and merchants in the Temple that Jesus would be on trial again, and if they wanted to exercise influence upon Pontius Pilate they should be there. He also told his attendants to spread the word amongst the followers of Barabbas that Jesus would be on trial and quite possibly might be used as a pawn in trade for Barabbas, so that the followers of Barabbas were advised to be present to have their voices heard in support of their hero. As he gave these instructions, Caiaphas even chuckled a little. It was all in the planning.

Next, he turned his attention to manipulating Pontius Pilate. The important thing was to make sure that Pilate became concerned, not with the actual works of Jesus, but with the influence He had upon the people and whether or not He would use that influence to the detriment of Rome. The primary factor, of course, was not so much something that was detrimental to Rome, as detrimental to Pontius Pilate. Any wisp of a rumor reaching the ears of Tiberius of difficulty in Judea, and Pontius Pilate would quite probably be immediately removed. Hence, the strategy for Caiaphas was to create fear of retribution by the emperor upon Pontius Pilate in the mishandling of the case of Jesus. The easy way out for Pontius Pilate would be to execute Him. There would never be any retribution from the emperor no matter how many people were executed. There would be retribution, however, if someone was not executed and subsequently became a problem. Mentally, Caiaphas almost said "Ah-ha!" The ploy with regard to Pontius Pilate had to be one of prevention and not one of commission.

Caiaphas walked on, a smile of anticipation lighting his features.

There was a large, boisterous crowd surrounding the antechamber of the Praetorian. As Jesus was led through crowd there was significant jeering. It became obvious that the crowd was opposed to Him. None of His many followers were present.

Caiaphas had also made an effort to ensure secrecy so that the general public would not be aware of what was transpiring, the trial of Jesus for His life.

As Caiaphas walked up to the crowd, he noticed the apostle John in the periphery of the crowd. He looked very carefully and noticed that none of the other apostles were there. He nodded to himself. "Good." He walked on.

As Jesus walked to the front of the crowd, chained and barely able to move, surrounded by guards, Pontius Pilate emerged from the Praetorian. He walked up to Jesus and looked at Him directly. Jesus stared back at him equally. He did not flinch. There was no fear in His eyes or His demeanor. Jesus stood before Pontius Pilate, certainly as an equal, if not a superior. It was not overbearing, it was merely a regal posture. There was nobility and an aura of latent power about Jesus. This was not lost on Pontius Pilate. He immediately sensed, as he had during his first encounter earlier with Jesus, that this was no ordinary person. He was almost differential in his tone of voice as he asked Jesus, "Who are you?"

"Where are you from?" But Jesus gave him no answer. Pilate therefore said to Him, "Do you refuse to speak to me? Do you not know that I have power to release you, and power to crucify you?" Jesus answered him, "You would have no power over me unless it had been given you from above; therefore the one who handed me over to you is guilty of a greater sin."

"Are you the king of the Jews?"

"Is that your own idea," Jesus asked, "or did others talk to you about me?"

"Am I a Jew?" Pilate replied. "Your own people and chief priests handed you over to me. What is it you have done?"

"My kingdom is not of this world." Jesus replied. "If it were, my servants would fight to prevent my arrest by the Jewish leaders. But now my kingdom is from another place."

"You are a king, then!" Pilate continued to ask.

Jesus answered, "You say that I am a king. In fact, the reason I was born and came into the world is to testify to the truth. Everyone on the side of truth listens to me."

"What is truth?" retorted Pilate.

Then he repeated the thought in his mind. What is Truth? What was Truth for Rome, for Jesus, and for Caiaphas?

There was a different truth for Rome, for Jesus and for Caiaphas.

For Rome, the truth was simple. It was whatever was good for Rome at the moment. It is was against Rome, it was not true.

For Jesus truth was what was, what is, and what was to be. Nothing was fabricated.

For Caiaphas, the only truth now was that Jesus had go. It didn't matter how or why, he had to go.

Pilate pondered truth now.

Pilate snorted, "What is truth?"

Glaring at Jesus, a shiver coursed through Pilate's body, and with it two fleeting thoughts: There is more to truth than the might of Rome; there is more to truth than Caiaphas' self-serving interpretation of Judaism.

Looking away, Pilate screamed to himself, "What is it?"

In all of the interrogation, Pontius Pilate and Jesus spoke in tones of voice that indicated respect for each other, and no obsequious subservience on the part of Jesus. As the interrogation continued, Pontius Pilate was continually impressed by the nobility of character of Jesus. In his mind, the words of his wife seemed to epitomize the reaction Jesus had upon him. Jesus was a just man. He was not an ordinary man. There was something unique about Him. He was certainly no criminal, and He was certainly not a threat to Rome. And then the counter-thought came in. But He could be! He had tremendous power and influence over significant numbers of people. They would follow Him. This rabble outside, Pontius Pilate suspected, had been assembled by Caiaphas in order to create the sense that Jesus did not have the support of the people. If it was true that He did not have the support, then He certainly was no threat. On the other hand, if Caiaphas had so engineered the crowd at the Praetorian, then he, Caiaphas, feared Jesus. That meant that Jesus was a threat to his power.

Pontius Pilate walked away from Jesus and stroked his chin as he pondered this problem. Why did Caiaphas fear Jesus? Was it religious, or political, or both? As he pondered, it came to him that Jesus was a threat to the status quo of the Jewish religion, speaking of a God who had compassion for His people where the common bond was love. The current status quo of the Jewish religion was one of supplication of a vengeful God, with fear as the primary motivation. Granted, sacrifice was made for supplication and remorse, but by-and-large, the Jewish religion was one rooted in the fear of their God. Jesus, on the other hand, was preaching a God of compassion and love. Could it be that Jesus personified the truth - God is love? Jesus spoke truth as it was.

Pontius Pilate immediately returned to the real world as he saw it. Caiaphas was trying to get him to issue the execution order of Jesus since Caiaphas could not. It would be easy for him to do so. It was not a case of becoming a tool in the machinations of Caiaphas, but rather a case of fulfilling his obligations as the Procurator of Judea. Truth for Rome was what was good for Rome. Peace and order was good for Rome. Perhaps Caiaphas was right that Jesus had to go. However, he differed with Caiaphas. There was no fault in Jesus.

As Pontius Pilate pondered the situation, the crowd became restless. They were stirred up by a pre-arranged signal from Annas. There were loud shouts of "Crucify Him! Crucify Him!"

The crowd almost went berserk. There were continual catcalls of "Crucify Him! Why are you not exercising your authority? He is a criminal." They even chanted "His blood be upon us and on our children!"

Pontius Pilate was somewhat shaken. Once again he thought that he would assuage the crowd by calling the commander of the guard, the Centurion Longinus, and instructing him to have Jesus taken to the punishment compound for the legion and to have Him whipped. He told the crowd that he was doing this. He was hoping that this would calm the crowd down. To some extent it did. He instructed Longinus to tell the torturer to lash Jesus with the cat of nine tails, forty times, twenty on the back and twenty on the front, but to avoid the face. Pontius Pilate did not want one of Jesus' eyes to be plucked out by the whip.

ROCCO LEONARD MARTINO

Chapter Seventeen
Condemned!

Jesus was taken to the punishing court for the Legion. He was tied to a pole and stripped of His garments. The brutal torturer/executioner picked up his heaviest whip and began lashing Jesus. Jesus did not make a sound. The pain must have been excruciating. After twenty lashes on the back He was turned and twenty lashes were administered to the front of His body. There was bleeding from many parts of His body. When it was done, the torturer/executioner was exhausted. Jesus was almost dead. But yet, when He was released from the whipping post, He stood erect. Though He was in severe pain, He showed no sign of any bending of His spirit.

The soldiers began to mock Him, calling Him "Your majesty, King" and shouting "Hail, King of the Jews!" They dressed Him in a purple robe. They took Him and crowned Him with a crown of thorns, striking it repeatedly into His brow until the blood ran down the side of His face. The soldiers derided Him, and yet He made no sound. They led Him back to Pontius Pilate in the plaza in front of the Praetorian. Jesus stumbled slightly but managed always to stand erect. As He emerged, the crowd began to jeer. There was no pity in this assembly. They wanted Him executed. They hated Him. The jeering reached a crescendo when Pontius Pilate entered from the Praetorian. He raised his hands and commanded them to be silent. The Roman soldiers stiffened and assumed menacing battle positions in order to cow the crowd. They did not succeed, but the crowd did become silent. Addressing the crowd, Pontius Pilate said, "What will you have me do with this man? I find Him to be just."

Once again the crowd shouted, "Crucify Him! Crucify Him!"

Pontius Pilate was startled. He did not want to crucify Jesus. But he would if he had to. He would try one more expedient. He remembered that during Passover, the Roman authorities quite often, as a gesture of good will, freed a criminal. He decided that he would offer the crowd a choice of Barabbas or Jesus to be freed. When he gave the crowd that choice they all screamed, "Barabbas! Barabbas!"

Pontius Pilate was stunned. He immediately gave orders to free Barabbas. That did not completely pacify the crowd.

Pontius Pilate looked up. The crowd was becoming more than restless; boisterous would be a more exact expression. He decided to show them his authority. He signaled to his guards and commanded them to bring a bowl of water. This was placed on a stand in front of the crowd to the side of Jesus. Pontius Pilate walked over to the bowl and washed his hands and raised them and let the water drip as he stated unequivocally, "I find no cause in this man." Pilate said to them, "Take Him yourselves and crucify Him; I find no case against Him." The Jews answered him, "We have a law, and according to that law He ought to die because He has claimed to be the Son of God."

Pilate looked directly at the crowd for a moment, then turned and looked directly at Jesus and then back at

THE CROSS OF VICTORY

the crowd. He shrugged his shoulders, threw up his hands, and issued the order to Longinus. "Crucify Him."

Pontius Pilate walked back into the Praetorian as Longinus led Jesus away.

'What is Truth?' thought Pilate in disgust. He grimaced as he noticed the broad grin on the face of Caiaphas. His strategy had worked. The crowd took on an almost festive air. They too had won!

As he was about to enter the Praetorian, a sudden thought came to Pontius Pilate. He turned and walked purposely back to the crowd, coming to a stop almost in front of Caiaphas, although he ignored him. Raising his voice in command to the Centurion Longinus, he gave instructions for a plaque to be placed on the upright of the crucifixion cross with the term, "This Is Jesus, King of the Jews." As he uttered the phrase, "King of the Jews," there was a roar from the crowd objecting. Pontius Pilate laughed, turned his back on them, and went into the Praetorian.

As Caiaphas walked away from the Praetorian, back to the Temple, he felt that he should be satisfied. He had achieved his objective of having Jesus condemned to execution. Yet there was a lingering sense that there was something special about Jesus. He well remembered the prophecy that He would rise from the dead. He wondered how Jesus would manage to rise from the dead if His body was eaten by animals. He knew that the common practice for the Romans was to leave the bodies on the cross until they were devoured or decayed. With that thought, Caiaphas put his mind at rest. There would be no resurrection. He walked hurriedly back to the Temple.

* * *

At the Praetorian, Joseph of Arimathea stood with Nicodemus. They watched sorrowfully as the guards began the crucifixion process. Surrounded by rioters and detractors hurling insults at Him, the soldiers immediately directed Jesus to pick up the cross member of His cross and carry it.

"Nicodemus, I am going to ask Pontius Pilate for permission to bury Jesus."

"Do you have a tomb that could be used?" asked Nicodemus.

"I have just completed a new tomb for myself," said Joseph. "I would be honored if Pontius Pilate would allow me to bury Jesus in that tomb.

"I am sure he will grant that request," said Nicodemus. "I think you should ask now."

Joseph of Arimathea nodded and walked over to a guard and asked to see Pontius Pilate.

In a short time, the guard returned and asked Joseph to accompany him. He was escorted into the meeting room inside the Praetorian. As he entered, Joseph realized he was being defiled but took this to be a small price to pay in performing this service for Jesus. If there was no burial, then the body of Jesus would be desecrated by animals or by decay as with others who were executed by crucifixion.

Pontius Pilate was most gracious in receiving Joseph of Arimathea. Joseph was a substantial citizen, well known to Pontius Pilate. He wondered what this distinguished citizen wanted.

Joseph immediately informed him of the request.

"Joseph," said Pontius Pilate, "you are most generous and gracious in offering your personal tomb to Jesus. I felt badly about condemning Him since I recognized Him to be a man without fault."

"Then why did you condemn Him to execution?" asked Joseph.

Pontius Pilate did not answer directly. He seemed to stare into space before looking directly at Joseph. "I felt that my hand was forced by the crowd. I was concerned that there would be a riot and I wasn't certain how far that would go. I gave the crowd a choice of Barabbas or Jesus and they chose Barabbas. I thought it best to proceed with the execution of Jesus." With a shrug, Pontius Pilate added, "Better one life than the many after a major riot if not rebellion."

Joseph remained silent. He had his own opinion. This was certainly not leadership, and certainly not governance, but he thought it wise to remain absolutely silent. He had achieved his objective. Jesus would be buried in a tomb.

Joseph thanked Pontius Pilate and took his leave. As he left, Pontius Pilate stood silently watching. His mind whirled with mixed emotions. There was something special about Jesus.

ROCCO LEONARD MARTINO

Chapter Eighteen
Informing the Disciples

John was overcome with sorrow when he heard the decision. The sheer injustice was beyond comprehension. The jeering of the crowd was of no consequence. They did not represent the Jewish people. John knew how Caiaphas had manipulated attendance and so the insults and cries for execution did not surprise him.

John hurried to find Mary and the other apostles to tell them the news. He assumed they were still at the house of John Mark where supper had been organized the night before. As he hurried to the house, the thought went through his mind that it seemed more like an eternity rather than less than twenty-four hours.

Supper had been superb. Jesus had shown His leadership and demonstrated His call to service both in His words but more importantly with the ritual of washing the feet of the apostles. Once again Peter had been taught an important lesson. With that thought a smile came on John's face. Peter was so sincere, and yet, in some sense almost the foil to drive home the lesson Jesus was teaching at the time. Poor Peter! He was full of love and admiration for Jesus. Jesus was wise to pick Peter to head His church.

Soon John arrived at the home of John Mark. He found Mary, Mary Magdalene, Lazarus, Peter, and most of the apostles in the upper room. He told them of decision to crucify Jesus. The minute he uttered the word Mary gave a scream of anguish. She burst into tears, her head bowed with the weight of her grief. In between deep sobs she said over and over "My little boy." John went over to her and embraced her, to comfort her. Gradually the sobs subsided, replaced by quiet weeping.

The other apostles were equally saddened. Peter, in particular was moved. John could see that he had wept copiously after his denial of Jesus in the courtyard of Caiaphas. He had fled back to this room, a haven for all of them. He started to speak, but stopped and remained silent. His face mirroring his grief. He sobbed quietly, muttering over and over "How could I have denied Him!" His grief was deep and obvious.

Gradually as the heavy sobs of Mary subsided, she looked at John and quietly said, "We must go to Him. He predicted this. He did not avoid it. He has made no move to stop it, even though He has the power. He is teaching us all an important lesson."

As she spoke, a memory flooded in of the prophecy of Simeon in the Temple when she and Joseph had taken Jesus to be circumcised. She still remembered the prediction words. "A sword of sorrow shall pierce your heart." All her life since she lived with the memory of those words in the expectation that they would come to fruition.

When the initial shock and grief had subsided somewhat, Peter said to those present, "We must go to Him." The other apostles immediately told Peter he could not. He would be recognized and perhaps killed. He was needed now to lead them with Jesus gone. They prevailed on him not to go. After a brief consultation, it was decided that only John and Lazarus would accompany Mary and Mary Magdalene. Peter and James would remain in the room with the others. There was great fear on the part of the apostles that they would be recognized and perhaps set upon by the unruly mob following Jesus.

They could not help but wonder why Jesus did not put an end to His suffering. They knew He had more power in the tip of His finger than the soldiers and the mob tormenting Him. But yet they remembered His teaching and prediction that this would happen. They also lived in the hope and expectation of His prediction that He would rise on the third day. As difficult as it was to believe this, they did! They had seen Jesus perform His miracles. They had seen Him raise Lazarus from the dead. They had seen the miracle of raising from the dead the son of the widow of Naim. And they had seen raising from the dead the daughter of the president of the Synagogue in Capernaum. Of course Jesus would rise from the dead.

In the meantime, however, Jesus was suffering terribly. He was sending a message to all mankind. It was His gift of love to everyone. His mission on earth had been the completion of the covenant between God and Adam in the garden. Forgiveness would henceforth be granted for the asking. The arms of God were open to all those who would enter and seek forgiveness. The only requirement was the request to be forgiven. It was not rules or dogma that prevailed, although they were important to be observed and followed, but rather love was to dominate the relationship of creature and creator. This would always inspire hope in the hearts of mankind. No matter what difficulty was being faced, forgiveness and love were never withdrawn. In the midst of their sorrow and anguish at the terrible suffering Jesus was undergoing, these thoughts stilled the pain in their hearts. There was the hope in love that all would end well.

    They took their leave of those who were not going with them, and departed.

Chapter Nineteen
Via Dolorosa

As soon as the final order to crucify was uttered by Pontius Pilate, the soldiers immediately began escorting Jesus towards the crossbeam of the cross which they were going to force Him to carry to the point of execution on Calvary Hill.

He bent to lift the crossbeam and He staggered a few steps and then fell. The soldiers whipped the fallen Jesus who struggled to rise but could not. The pathway was through the winding streets of Jerusalem from the courtyard of the Praetorian to Cavalry, the place of execution. It was not a significant distance, but for someone who had been beaten unmercifully as Jesus had, carrying a heavy cross, it was a difficult journey. Jesus stumbled and the Roman soldiers, wanting to ensure that Jesus would remain alive so He could be crucified, conscripted someone from the people in the street to help Him carry the cross.

Looking at the crowd surrounding Jesus, they selected a strong looking young man as a potential helper to carry the cross.

"Who are you?" the Centurion asked.

"I am called Simon. I come from Cyrene. I was attracted by the noise."

"Do you know this man?" asked the Roman Centurion.

"No. I came to Jerusalem for Passover, and hearing the noise, came over to see what it was."

"Good. Then help this man carry His cross," ordered the Centurion.

Seeing a look of defiance on the face of Simon, the Centurion Longinus barked, "Do it!"

Simon was taken aback, and resisted briefly before recognizing the fact that he could not win against the dictates of a Roman Centurion. He looked askance at Jesus, and not knowing anything about the situation, wondered how such a man could come to be so brutalized. And yet, despite His weakness, and despite the terrible pain that He obviously had racking His body, Jesus still had an upright bearing and a nobility of stature that impressed Simon. This was no ordinary man.

Simon knelt under the crossbeam and gradually he and Jesus raised it. The Procession restarted on its way to Calvary.

The crowd dispersed around Him, jeering and taunting Him that if He were the son of God then He should be exercising His power to rescue Himself. Throughout all of this, Jesus maintained a regal bearing, saying nothing, making no sound.

Caiaphas gave immediate instructions to his attendants to keep the crowd stirred up so that they would follow Jesus and ensure that the followers of Jesus would be separated from Him, so they wouldn't always know what was happening to Him. Jesus had to be executed before His followers and supporters even knew it happened.

There was still a crowd, although somewhat diminished, surrounding Jesus, jeering and taunting Him, when Joseph and Nicodemus caught up to the procession.

THE CROSS OF VICTORY

The boisterous crowd had thinned out markedly, but Jesus was still almost surrounded by a jeering group shouting, "If you can perform miracles, then save yourself." Or they screamed "Where are the angels to come to your aid?" Or "If you are a King, where is your power?"

Jesus made no reaction to the taunts meant to torment Him. He looked straight ahead, carrying His cross beam with the help of Simon of Cyrene. It was Simon who shouted back at the crowd to be silent and respect the man He was helping. Simon was visibly impressed with the courage and calm with which Jesus carried His cross and bore His pain. The insults did not seem to bother Him. Simon heard Jesus mutter a few times, "Father, forgive them. They know not what they do."

Jesus stumbled two more times, but it was Simon of Cyrene who helped Him regain His balance. Even the crowd was impressed with the nobility of His bearing. He was obviously suffering. He made no sound or sign of this.

The way was short, but long in many ways. There were few on-lookers, since many were in preparation for the Passover. There was some curiosity occasionally, with regard to the noise of the jeering followers, but on the whole, the procession did not attract a following. The triumphant entry of Jesus into Jerusalem only five days before where He had been surrounded by His followers was replaced by this procession towards His execution where He was surrounded by His detractors and enemies.

As the procession continued, His detractors gradually broke off, many of them then proceeding to the Temple to take on their responsibilities as money-changers and merchants of lambs and doves. Had they not been so occupied, they would have followed Jesus to the execution point and watched Him die.

As the crowd gradually dwindled, the nature of the procession became apparent to on-lookers, and a number came to watch. Some left to inform the followers of Jesus as to what had been decided. Soon the followers of Jesus assembled by John began to surround the sorrowful procession. They couldn't believe the condition of Jesus. His body showed where the lash had struck. Blood oozed from His wounds. On His head the crown of thorns bit into His brow. Blood trickled down the side of His face, yet, despite the obvious pain and debility, He still walked purposefully, carrying the crossbeam of His cross. Jesus was unbowed.

When John and Mary came upon the procession, on seeing the obvious suffering of Jesus, Mary gasped. She was stunned at His appearance. A scream escaped her. It reverberated in the air, a scream of absolute anguish. "My son! My son! My son!" For a moment it stunned the crowd into silence. Then they shrugged it off and continued their heckling of Jesus. The crown of thorns was cutting deep gouges in His head. Blood dripped down His face. His body was covered in cuts and flaps of bleeding skin from His back. Yet He struggled with the cross. Mary sobbed uncontrollably, yet, in a place where Jesus would not see her. Over and over she said, "My son. My son. What have they done to you?"

The sound of other sobs could soon be heard even in the noise of the crowd.

After the initial shock wore off, the sobbing became subdued. The followers of Jesus gradually elbowed away most of the detractors and surrounded

Jesus as if to give Him comfort by their presence. Some began to openly cry. At one point, a group of women assembled and Jesus stopped. They were weeping profusely. Jesus said to them, "Daughters of Jerusalem, do not weep for me, but weep for yourselves and for your children. For the days are surely coming when they will say, 'Blessed are the barren, and the wombs that never bore, and the breasts that never nursed.' Then they will begin to say to the mountains, 'Fall on us'; and to the hills, 'Cover us.' For if they do this when the wood is green, what will happen when it is dry?"

Then the procession wended its way until they came to the crucifixion point. On Calvary Hill there were three uprights already in place. The one in the center was for Jesus. Already affixed at the top was the designation "Jesus, King of the Jews" as ordered by Pontius Pilate.

ROCCO LEONARD MARTINO

Chapter Twenty
Crucifixion

As they came to the upright, Jesus was thrown down by the soldiers and Simon was dismissed. As Jesus lay there, on top of the crossbeam, Simon looked down upon Him. He did not know this man, but he was torn by pity at the suffering and obvious great pain and anguish that Jesus had suffered and was still suffering. He was impressed by the demeanor of Jesus. Throughout, He had made no complaint, given no threats or curses, and unlike other criminals, did not engage in any kind of recrimination of the soldiers. He had suffered quietly, with great dignity.

As Simon left, he could not help but sense that he had been part of something very important, even though he did not truly understand what it was.

Prior to beginning the process of nailing Jesus to the cross, He was stripped of all of His garments. These articles the Legionaries would draw lots for after they had completed the process of crucifixion.

The soldiers roughly stretched the arms of Jesus on each side of the center of the crossbeam. One took a long nail and took the right wrist of Jesus and nailed it to the cross. Jesus gasped in pain as the nail drove through His wrist into the crossbeam. The soldier wielding the mallet took no notice and continued to hammer until he was certain that Jesus was firmly affixed to the crossbeam by His right wrist.

When this was done, he proceeded to take the left wrist of Jesus and repeat the process.

In the usual fashion, as the crossbeam was about to be raised, Jesus was offered wine mixed with gall. When He tasted it, He rejected it. Then the Legionaries proceeded to put ropes around the crossbeam and affix it to the upright and lift Jesus into a cross position, all of his weight now coming to rest on His wrists nailed to the cross.

When the crossbeam was in position, the Legionaries took His feet and, placing one upon the other at the footrest on the upright, nailed His feet to the upright. This gave some relief to the excruciating pain being suffered by Jesus as His weight now bore on the footrest and not totally on His wrists. His arms, however, were extending upwards and this placed great pressure on His chest, making breathing laborious and difficult.

The pain, the flogging, the crowning with thorns, and the trip carrying the crossbeam of His cross had exhausted Jesus almost to the point of death.

Longinus, who had participated in many executions, looked at Jesus and in his mind estimated that He would soon be dead.

In the midst of His excruciating pain and suffering, Jesus still prayed for forgiveness for His tormenters and executioners. "Father," He prayed, "forgive them for they know not what they do."

Longinus, who heard Him, was struck by the nobility and true-to-life message of Jesus by His words and by His suffering today. Jesus was certainly no ordinary man, concluded Longinus. He would have to look further into this.

For now, however, he would follow his orders to complete the execution of Jesus.

While this had been proceeding, other members of the squad of Legionaries had been proceeding with the execution of two thieves, one of each side of Jesus. They were not nailed to the crosspiece. Their arms were affixed to these with ropes. Then the crosspieces in turn were raised and placed into position. As with Jesus, the crosspiece was affixed to the upright with heavy ropes and with support from a rope hanging down from the top of the upright.

One of the criminals who was hanged there kept deriding Him and saying, "Are you not the Messiah? Save yourself and us!" But the other rebuked Him, saying, "Do you not fear God, since you are under the same sentence of condemnation? And we indeed have been condemned justly, for we are getting what we deserve for our deeds, but this man has done nothing wrong." Then he said, "Jesus, remember me when you come into your Kingdom." Jesus replied, "Truly I tell you, today you will be with me in Paradise."

When Jesus saw His mother and the disciple whom He loved standing beside her, He said to His mother, "Woman, here is your son." Then He said to the disciple, "Here is your mother." And from that hour the disciple, John, took her into his own home.

Shortly after this exchange, life began to ebb rapidly.

Jesus, crying with a loud voice, said, "Father, into your hands I commend my spirit."

As Jesus hung, dying on the cross, the skies darkened. At the moment He died, there was a terrible roll of thunder. In the Temple, the veil was torn asunder. The worshippers in the Temple knew that something had happened of great import.

Caiaphas had preceded to the hill to ensure that Jesus was finally crucified. As he approached the cross, he had not expected to see that Jesus' head was hanging. Apparently He must have died rather quickly. He was not surprised, taking into account the terrible flogging He had endured. The darkened skies impressed Caiaphas with the thought that something special had happened. As he stood looking up at the head of Jesus, covered in blood from the thorns that had pierced His forehead, he sighed. The thought went through his head, this man was special. Whether He was the son of God or not, and he believed not, there was no question Jesus was not an ordinary man. He must have been insane. Caiaphas understood that Jesus was brilliant, as evidenced by the reports of the manner in which He had discoursed and commented upon the scriptures in various Synagogues around the country, and in His disputes with the scholars in the Temple. Still He must have been insane. To have claimed to have been the son of God and to have carried through the charade with this terrible way of dying was certainly not the behavior of a normal human being. How He managed to cure people of various illnesses was beyond his understanding. It was trickery of some kind. Sadly, Caiaphas shook his head. He had pity upon Jesus because Jesus was a human being. He had no pity beyond that since in his opinion Jesus had brought it all upon Himself. He turned and walked away. Then he stopped. He had been told that Joseph of Arimathea had requested that Jesus be buried in his tomb. The thought suddenly emerged in his mind that the tomb had to be guarded lest the apostles would steal the body and claim that Jesus had risen from the dead. He would have to secure the approval of Pontius Pilate for that. Suddenly energized, he strode vigorously away.

The Centurion Longinus looked upon the sky and realized that it became necessary to break the legs of those who had been crucified so that they would die. He proceeded to do so with the thieves on either side of Jesus. When he came to Jesus, he saw that He was comatose, and perhaps already dead. It surprised him since He had died, if He had died, so quickly. Taking his spear he thrust it into the side. Immediately blood and water gushed. Longinus knew that Jesus was dead.

He noticed that the mother of Jesus and one of His disciples, the young John, were at the foot of the cross. He should have realized that Jesus was dead from the sobbing. His heart was touched deeply by the sight of the grieving Mary, the mother of Jesus. Quietly he turned away and signaled to the Legionaries to lower the crossbeam so that Jesus could be removed from the cross. This was exceptional but he had been instructed by a message from Pontius Pilate that Jesus was to be buried in a nearby grotto. He stood there watching Jesus lowered from the cross and the tenderness with which His body was received by His mother, Mary Magdalene, and by His apostle John. He noticed Joseph of Arimathea standing there and assumed that it was his tomb that was being used to receive the body of Jesus. He gave instructions to the Legionaries to assist in moving the body of Jesus to the tomb. He continued to watch as the body of Jesus was tenderly washed, covered with myrrh, and then wrapped. He continued to observe as Jesus was placed in the tomb and visualized the loving care with which His face was covered with the burial cloth.

ROCCO LEONARD MARTINO

Chapter Twenty-One
The Wake

They took Jesus down from the cross. The process began by removing the spike nail that attached His feet to the upright. Then the Legionaries lowered the crossbeam. As the body was lowered, John and Lazarus supported the body of Jesus so it would not be mangled. When the crossbeam was on the ground, the Legionaries came over and removed the large spike nails attaching His wrists to the crossbeam. The Legionaries seemed subdued as they did this. They knew there was something different about this man. They were well aware of the disputes prior to the crucifixion. They had seen the Procurator wash his hands of the blood of this just man. And yet he had issued the order to have Him crucified. They wondered; but they were soldiers. They obeyed orders. Still, they were thinking men.

As promised, the servants of Joseph Arimathea were present. It was they who had brought with them containers with water, washing clothes, spices, and a large burial cloth for the body. When the crossbeam was fully on the ground, John removed the crown of thorns from the head of Jesus. With the help of the servants, John and Lazarus laid the body of Jesus on the coarse preparation sheet. With Mary and Mary Magdalene, they proceeded to wash the body. Then they laid out the burial cloth, covered in with a liberal coating of burial, spices, and then moved the body as tenderly and gently as possible onto the burial cloth. More spices were spread on the body; the arms of Jesus were crossed so that His hands rested within each other. The burial cloth was lovingly wrapped around Jesus. With the help of the Legionaries, John and Lazarus carried the body of Jesus the short distance to the tomb originally prepared for the body of Joseph of Arimathea. Once there, they entered the tomb and lovingly placed the wrapped body onto the burial stone within the tomb. Each of them, then, including Joseph, stood quietly and softly looking upon the face of Jesus, perhaps for the last time as they did so. Each in his own way remembered the goodness of Jesus, always giving of Himself and never seeking anything other than love and acceptance. Each in turn left, until only Mary remained. Then she knelt and embraced Jesus once more. A sigh escaped her and she kissed His cheek. She whispered "I love you my son. Rest in peace." Then she rose, covered the face of Jesus with the burial cloth, and exited from the tomb.

Just about this time the contingent of sixteen Legionaries sent by Pontius Pilate to guard the tomb arrived. They were under the command of the Centurion Polonius. John went over to him and asked why they were there. The Centurion replied they had been sent by Pontius Pilate at the request of Caiaphas. Apparently Caiaphas was concerned the body would be stolen and false rumors would be circulated about the resurrection of Jesus. With this guard that would be impossible to accomplish.

John nodded. He quietly said to himself, if Jesus wanted to rise from the dead, and He surely would, neither sixteen soldiers nor sixteen thousand would stop Him.

When Mary, the mother of Jesus, Mary Magdalene, Joseph of Arimathea, and John emerged

THE CROSS OF VICTORY

from the tomb, John asked for their help in moving the stone across the face of tomb. Polonius was pleased to agree. Polonius signaled to the Legionaries to help John and Lazarus roll the stone in front of the tomb.

Sorrowfully, Mary and the other followers of Jesus stood before the tomb. Jesus was gone! After a few more moments of quiet sobbing, they left.

After the soldiers had rolled the stone to cover the front of the tomb Joseph took his leave of the others and set out for his home. His path took him past the Temple. By chance, Caiaphas came out of the Temple as Joseph went by. They both stopped to talk.

"Terrible tragedy," began Caiaphas, "He had so much to offer, but chose to die ignominiously on a cross like a common criminal. What a waste!"

Joseph kept his temper. Looking directly at Caiaphas, Joseph answered him quietly but with a fervor that surprised the Chief Priest.

"You are wrong, Caiaphas! The death of Jesus will resound through the centuries to come. His followers will take up the cross as a symbol, of His conquest of evil. It will become a Cross of Victory - victory over sin, victory over death, and victory over despair." Joseph stopped in deep thought, his emotions almost overcoming him. Then he added in a soft yet strong voice.

"Oh you fool, Caiaphas. Could you not see who He is for even in death He lives." Joseph sadly shook his head as Caiaphas remained silent. "In centuries to come, the Cross of Victory will prevail as a symbol of hope, love and eternal life."

With that Joseph walked away, leaving a crestfallen Caiaphas standing there.

The soldiers began their bivouac for the night, ranging themselves in groups of four for continual guarding of the tomb. When Polonius was satisfied with the arrangements, he placed a senior Legionary in charge and left.

Mary turned to Mary Magdalene and said, "It is late for you and Lazarus to return to Bethany. Why not spend the night with us? We have plenty of room. The home of John Mark is big enough for all of us. Come."

Looking toward Lazarus, Mary Magdalene nodded, and they left for the home of John Mark. The other apostles, including Peter, were waiting in the upper room.

A short time later, they arrived at the home of John Mark, and proceeded to the upper room. They did not have to say a word. The marked sorrowful looks on their faces were enough to tell everyone that Jesus was dead. John proceeded to tell them all of the gift of his personal tomb by Joseph of Arimathea for the burial of Jesus. He then relayed information concerning the contingent of soldiers sent by Pontius Pilate to guard the tomb. This resulted in some brief humor even in the midst of their deep sorrow. They all believed that Jesus would rise on the third day. They didn't know how or when on the third day, but they believed He would.

Rapidly the women put together some dinner for the group. As the sun went down and the Sabbath began, they began to speak of Jesus, and what He had accomplished in His ministry during three years.

It was Peter who led the discussion. He seemed to fit automatically into the role of leader in the absence of Jesus. "Jesus has created a lasting change to our religion," he began. "He taught us, and He wants us to teach others, that none of us are without sin. That does not condemn us. We can seek forgiveness and it will be freely granted. It will be granted out of love on our part of God, and love of God for us. It is love that Jesus has taught us."

With that Peter remained silent. It was Matthew who spoke up. "How can you say that, Peter, when so many glorified at His crucifixion. You believe they will be forgiven for what they did."

John, who stood at the foot of the cross, and heard Jesus beg forgiveness, replied. "Matthew, I heard Jesus ask His father to forgive them for they know not what they do. Anyone and everyone, no matter what they have done, who repent and seek forgiveness for their sins shall be forgiven."

Matthew nodded in understanding. "Yes, I can just hear Jesus doing it." After a short pause he continued, "I have been too long with a rigid set of rules that govern my behavior and everything. I have been too long with a rigid requirement of sacrifice for forgiveness of my sins. Finally, I have been too long fearful of the vengeance of God. I welcome this change in recognizing that we have a loving God who recognizes the realities of life that we are all sinners. His arms are open to all those who seek forgiveness out of love, in turn, for God, with their hearts full of rejection for their sins of the past."

Matthew paused again and looked directly at Peter. "Did I get it right this time?" He asked.

Peter smiled. "Yes you did."

Then they all began to quietly ponder in their own private thoughts what Jesus had meant to them. Throughout this quiet time Mary gradually stopped her quiet sobbing. They continued to talk until late in the night.

They spent the Sabbath together. Once more they continued their memories of Jesus. It was Mary who reminded them that Jesus had a tremendous sense of humor. While His preaching often was on a serious topic, and while His miracles cured people of major illness, or brought them back to life, people rarely saw Him relaxed. Jesus loved to mingle with His friends. Quite often when He was under attack His answer had hidden humor in the reply. For instance, Mary mentioned the sally with the Pharisees who presented Jesus with a coin bearing the face of Caesar Augustus, asking if it was right to pay taxes to the Romans. Jesus then made His very famous reply, "Render unto Caesar that which is Caesar's, and unto God that which is God's." Taken in the context of humor, even in the midst of direct and important purpose, the hidden humor was obvious. Jesus could have said, "You must be kidding. This coin belongs to Caesar. Give it to him. God has no use for such trinkets. He seeks only your love, not your trinkets."

Then Mary recounted stories of Jesus' first miracle. Jesus had accompanied her to the wedding feast in Cana. When the wine ran out she cajoled Jesus into helping the groom. With a deep smile, He told the stewards to fill the empty skins with water, and then to serve it. Everyone was ecstatic. The water had become wine, better than any wine served previously.

With a smile on her face, Mary recounted the situation of the fig tree which had not produced good fruit. Jesus had apparently commanded the tree to produce good fruit, and when it did not He condemned

THE CROSS OF VICTORY

it. Mary reminded them that Jesus was showing His sense of humor while He taught a lesson in obedience.

It was John who quietly raised the point that Jesus always insulated His followers from His suffering. Even when He was in deep anguish in the garden, He suffered alone. While He teased His apostles about not staying awake, He really did not invite them to share His grief.

John had watched all the proceedings to which Jesus had been subjected. "No one took His part," said John. "He stood alone before Annas, Caiaphas, the Sanhedrin, Pontius Pilate, Herod, and finally Pontius Pilate a second time." John stopped and remained in deep thought for a few moments before continuing. "At all times, He stood His ground. At all times they could find no guilt in Him. After constant challenging by Caiaphas, He finally said, "You have said it yourself; nevertheless I tell you, hereafter you will see the Son of Man sitting at the right hand of power, and coming on the clouds of Heaven."

The room became very quiet as John stopped. All in their own thoughts suddenly realized the divinity of Jesus. After a prolonged pause, John continued. "Jesus went through His entire suffering period alone – the flogging, carrying His cross, the crucifixion, and His death. Alone. No one came to His defense. No-one offered to carry His burden." With a quiet sob, John ended with the words. "He did it all for us. He died alone on a lonely cross."

And so they passed the day. Lurking at all times in the undercurrent of their discussions was the sad fact that Jesus was not with them.

Mary Magdalene and Lazarus stayed with them for the Sabbath, and agreed to spend the night as well. They all retired early to be ready for whatever would come tomorrow, the third day.

Chapter Twenty-Two
Jesus is Risen!

It was the first day of the week, as Mary Magdalene wended her way to the tomb of Jesus. It was the third day since His execution. Her heart was heavy in the sorrow that He was gone.

As she approached the tomb, she was surprised to see that the guards were gone. She was startled to see that the stone was rolled away. She gasped. With her hand at her mouth, she approached slowly and cautiously. Walking up to the tomb, she peered inside. It was empty! She gave a sudden deep inhalation, and screamed, "He is risen!"

Suddenly she heard her name called, "Mary, Mary." She turned and saw a man standing in the garden. Again He called, "Mary, Mary."

She drew in her breath. Her hand flew to her mouth. It was Jesus! Then as Jesus smiled at her, she gasped again. "You are risen!"

ROCCO LEONARD MARTINO

Reviews of *The Resurrection: A Criminal Investigation* ...

"So yesterday I finally had time to pick up your book and the only problem was I couldn't stop reading it. Congratulations and thanks for my wonderful experience. You really captured the essence of our faith in a manner easy for all to follow. Your book is an excellent tool for the Year of Faith.......Your summary of leadership was also right on target!"
   -Tim Flanagan, Founder and Chair, Catholic Leadership Institute

"Dr. Martino paints Tribune Quintus as a savvy detective assigned by the Roman Emperor to undertake seriously the apparent disappearance of the body of the crucified criminal Jesus of Nazareth. Filled with tension and mysterious details, the book locks our attention. I found it hard to put the book aside....the story finally shines into the face, and the soul, of us readers an important serious question....does that reveal the crucified Criminal Jesus of Nazareth as ALIVE? And if so, how important is that to all of us? The novel, breathless at times, rings with the Good News of the Risen Jesus."
   -Rev. George Aschenbrenner, S.J., Jesuit Center, Wernersville, Pennsylvania; Rector Emeritus, University of Scranton

"Throughout history many have attempted, well intentioned or otherwise, to augment or rewrite the gospel record of the life, death and resurrection of Jesus Christ: Gnostics in the early centuries of Christianity and modern movie producers being two examples. In most cases artistic license, or worse deliberate theological distortion, trumped truth and accuracy. A clear exception is "The Resurrection: A Criminal Investigation..." Faith is not being challenged; it is enhanced. Doctor Martino has expertly crafted an imaginary scenario of the events not recorded in Scripture of the happenings surrounding the death and resurrection of Jesus. The story is not only plausible but compelling. The characters with familiar names are vividly portrayed. The reader easily is carried back two thousand years to contemplate, through the eyes of a Roman Tribune, the Paschal Mystery, and become better for the experience."

-Paul Peterson, Professor of Theology,
Archdiocese of Philadelphia

"Believe it! For 99 cents, I was able to read, perhaps, one of the most important books I will ever read! Once I started, I couldn't stop until finished, less than a day! For me personally, it seemed to give me what I had been searching for all my life!....This is a must-read for anybody who would like to learn how the investigation of an individual should be conducted...before...they were crucified....Thank you Dr. Martino for satisfying my personal need for closure...and for justice to prevail, at least legally..."

-Glenda A. Bixler, Editor, GABixlerReviews

"Leaving to others the subtleties of biblical criticism, Dr. Martino leads us through an engaging series of interviews conducted by a persistent but sensitive Roman tribune seeking the answer to why the tomb of Jesus was empty. The author gives expression to his vivid faith and his taste for logic and reasoning, treating us to a couple of imaginative surprises at the end."
    -Peter Kearney, Biblical Scholar

"This book brings commonality to theology."
    -Dr. Patrick McCarthy, KMOb

"I am reading your book myself and find it thoroughly gripping and very well researched....your book is a real page turner....it is a deeply inspirational work."
    -Gerard O'Sullivan, PhD, Vice President for Academic Affairs, Neumann University

"A vivid portrayal of the most time-less events of our salvation history... the empty tomb elicits gripping attention, lingering wonderment and thanksgiving."
    -Dr. Robert Capizzi, FACP, FASCO, Co-Founder, President, Chief Medical Officer, CharlestonPharma, LLC

"I wanted to let you know that I just finished your latest book, The Resurrection. I thought it would be a fitting read for Holy Week. Thank you for writing it! Even

though I'm a believer, it always helps to have my beliefs reinforced, and your wonderful book certainly did that for me. I enjoyed your creative approach and liked the way you brought the characters to life. Every doubter of Christ's life, death and resurrection should read this book."
                    -Stafford Worley, Co-Founder, Worens Group

"THE RESURRECTION. What a marvelous experience. Congratulations! I thoroughly enjoyed it. You really integrated everything in a most engaging way."
                    -Rev. Dominic Maruca, S.J., Professor Emeritus, Pontifical Gregorian University of Rome

"I read your book, 'Resurrection', and it is the best yet. It's fascinating to see how one uses logic to arrive at the same conclusions that the rest of us arrive at by faith."
    -Dr. Stephen Schuster, University of Pennsylvania Health Systems.

"I enjoyed reading it very much. The way the author told the story kept my interest in the factual details of what really happened to our crucified Lord. I learned so much of why Jesus was unjustly murdered. Reading your book strengthens me in my own fundamental faith and beliefs in the agony and suffering of Jesus."
    -Rev. John Snyder, S.J., Former Board Member, Pontifical Gregorian University of Rome

"...just as Mel Gibson's movie The Passion has forever changed how I feel about the ministry and painful death of Christ...The Resurrection has changed how I...feel about the politics behind Christ's conviction to death...I really enjoyed this...and foresee a film version..."
   -James Longon, Entrepreneur

"I must congratulate you on your page-turner THE RESURRECTION. It is fascinating, beautifully written and – well brilliant! I enjoyed every minute of it. It deserves a wide readership...a potent force for evangelization. Thanks for writing it..."
   -Patricia Lynch, Avid Reader

ROCCO LEONARD MARTINO

Reviews of *Christianity: A Criminal Investigation* . . .

"I have read over Christianity: A Criminal Investigation of the Motivation, Structure, Growth, and Threat to Rome by Dr. Martino. There are no doctrinal problems with it."
  -*Rev. Robert A. Pesarchick, STD, Academic Dean, Theological Seminary and Professor of Systematic Theology, St. Charles Borromeo Seminary*

"A very readable story, this could well be the basic text for a formation program. All Christian principles presented in a relaxed manner through the marvels of a fascinating narrative."
  -*Professor John J. Schrems, PhD, Professor Emeritus, University of Pennsylvania*

"Christianity" is to Dr. Martino's previous historical novel, "Resurrection," as the Acts of the Apostles is to Luke's Gospel. Although the genres are different, in each case the second opus builds masterfully on the first. Highly imagined, well described scenes, populated by compelling characters, real and fictional, present a plausible understanding of the beginnings of Christianity in Rome - a historical fact confirming the ongoing presence of the Risen Christ in His Church. Readers,

even more so, of this book will be especially drawn to Quintus, the quintessential military officer and the embodiment of ethics, who even after a lifetime of experience investigating the faith in Jesus Christ is unable to grasp the ultimate significance of the Resurrection. Mark, with a prominent role in the story, will record Jesus saying: "This is the time of fulfillment. The kingdom of God is at hand. Repent and believe in the gospel." Readers, with the grace of God, can grow in their faith, reading about Quintus struggling to go beyond his Roman mindset, to achieve what he sees in these first Christians, *metanoia* – their determination to advance the kingdom of God, a new creation – what Paul wrote to the Corinthians: "So whoever is in Christ is a new creation: the old things have passed away; behold, new has come."
   -Paul Peterson, Professor of Theology,
   Archdiocese of Philadelphia

"A refreshingly unique perspective on the beginning of Christianity. The characters' testimony of events from a different approach makes the reader delve yet again into the basis of their belief or non-belief."
   -Anne Condello, Avid Reader

CPSIA information can be obtained
at www.ICGtesting.com
Printed in the USA
LVOW04s0345070616
491420LV00025B/741/P